THE CAMBORNE KILLINGS

SALLY RIGBY

Storm

Copyright © Sally Rigby, 2024

The moral right of the author has been asserted.

To request permissions, contact the publisher at rights@stormpublishing.co

Ebook ISBN: 978-1-80508-631-4
Paperback ISBN: 978-1-80508-633-8

Cover design: Lisa Horton
Cover images: Arcangel, Shutterstock

Published by Storm Publishing.
For further information, visit:
www.stormpublishing.co

PROLOGUE

'Blast,' the woman muttered as she sat in her worn comfy chair with a mug of hot chocolate, ready to watch her favourite TV programme. She glanced across at Maud, her old tabby cat curled up next to her and who'd opened a single eye at the sound of her voice. 'Who on earth can be at the door? It's gone nine.' Her heart pounded slightly. It was unusual to have visitors this late.

She placed her mug on the coffee table and headed out of the small lounge. She opened the front door and standing before her was a man, fear and desperation etched across his face. He was tall, about six-foot-two, with close-cut grey hair.

'Yes?' she said, an uneasy chill creeping up her spine.

'I'm so sorry to bother you,' he said, his voice wavering slightly. 'I've had an accident down the road.' He turned to point in the direction from where he came.

'Are you okay?' She looked him up and down. There didn't appear to be any blood.

'Yeah, but I hit a dog. I jumped out of my car to see if it was injured but it ran off... I think it went into your barn.'

'What sort of dog is it?' she asked, her mind racing. Was it Jack, her neighbour's Labrador which was often out roaming the streets?

'A small terrier, I think. It was hard to see. It happened so quickly. I can't believe it. I need to make sure it's okay or take it to the vet or back to its owner—'

'Try not to worry,' the woman said interrupting him, before he went into full panic mode. 'And you think it went into my barn?'

'Well, yes, over there,' he said, pointing at the outbuilding.

The door should have been shut but glancing across the drive she could see it was open. Perhaps the latch hadn't caught when she'd put the chickens to bed earlier.

'Let's go and see.'

She slipped on her shoes, which were by the front door, and together they headed towards the barn.

'Should I call the police?' the man asked. 'I know you have to report accidents.'

'We'll wait until we've checked. You might've only startled the dog and it went into the barn to recover.'

'The roads are so winding round here. That's why I didn't see it,' the man said, his voice echoing in the quiet night.

'You're not local then?'

'No, I'm visiting friends for the weekend. It's so beautiful here.'

'Yes, you're right about that. And quiet. Whereabouts do your friends live? I might know them.'

'They're in Penzance. I was out for a drive admiring the scenery. I know it's nighttime, but it's still light enough to enjoy.' He paused for a moment. 'Maybe that's why I didn't see the dog because I wasn't concentrating on the road.'

'Don't worry,' she said, attempting to soothe him. 'Follow me.'

'Thanks. I'm very sorry to disturb your evening.'

'It's fine. Where are you from?' she asked, hoping the small talk would ease his tension.

'A few miles outside of London.'

'Much noisier than here, I suspect,' the woman said with a chuckle.

'You're not wrong about that. I wish I could live here, but London's where my work is.'

They reached the barn and walked in. She glanced around and nothing seemed to be out of place.

'The dog doesn't appear to be in here unless it's hiding underneath the hay by the mower over there,' she said, nodding to the corner of the barn.

She headed over and bent down to take a look. There was nothing but shadows and the cold barn floor.

As she turned to face her companion, her breath caught in her throat. The man stood eerily still, his face devoid of any warmth or emotion. In his hand he gripped a baseball bat, his knuckles white from the sheer force of his hold.

Her heart hammered in her chest as she tried to comprehend the situation.

Where had the bat come from?

Had he hidden in it the barn?

But before she could react, he swung the bat with a swift and calculated motion and the sound of wood connecting with her head made a sickening crack.

She crumpled to the ground, her vision blurring as pain exploded through her skull. The world spun around, and the cold damp floor pressed against her cheek.

The man loomed over her, his shadow casting a menacing darkness across her barely conscious form. With a chilling calmness he propped her up against the rough hay bales, her body limp and unresponsive.

The glint of a knife caught her fading vision as he pulled it from his pocket.

'Say your goodbyes,' he whispered in her ear, his breath hot against her skin.

He plunged the knife deep into her heart and the silence of the barn suffocated her final, feeble gasps for air, as the life drained from her body.

ONE

SUNDAY, 14 JULY

Detective Sergeant Matt Price strolled into his favourite café in the centre of Penzance and scanned the room to see if his friend and ex-colleague, Detective Constable Ellie Naylor, had arrived. The café was a quaint, cosy spot with rustic wooden tables and chairs, and walls covered with local artwork depicting the stunning Cornish coastline. The aroma of freshly brewed coffee and homemade pastries filled the air, creating a warm and inviting atmosphere. He'd been both surprised and delighted when she'd contacted him and asked if she could visit him in Cornwall and stay for a couple of weeks.

Although they'd kept in touch sporadically since he'd moved there, she hadn't suggested visiting. He'd assumed it was because work had been hectic and in her spare time she was with her boyfriend, Dean. He could tell by her voice when they'd spoken that something had happened but all she said was that she needed a break and would fill him in on everything when they were together.

He would have invited her to stay with him, his parents and young daughter, Dani, but they were absolutely full to the brim.

Instead, he'd found a reasonably priced bed-and-breakfast close by, and Ellie had booked in there. He couldn't see her at first until suddenly, he caught sight of someone waving in the corner. He headed over and as he got closer sucked in a breath. She didn't look like the Ellie he'd left in Lenchester. Her usually vibrant, shoulder-length blonde hair appeared dull and lifeless, and her once sparkling blue eyes seemed tired and distant. Her face was drawn, and she looked to have lost quite a lot of weight, making her delicate features even more pronounced.

When he reached the table, she jumped up and gave him a large hug. 'It's so good to see you,' she said, her voice trembling.

'You, too,' he said releasing her and sitting down. 'I wasn't expecting a visit because the last time we spoke you mentioned being so busy.'

Ellie glanced down, her fingers nervously fiddling with the sleeve of her oversized sweater. 'Well, that's because things have changed.' A shadow crossed her face, and Matt sensed that there was much she'd left unspoken.

'I'll order us something to drink, and then you tell me more about it. Still coffee with milk, no sugar?'

'Yes, that would be great. But with oat milk, please.' Ellie's lips curved up slightly, but the expression didn't quite reach her eyes.

'Okay. I'll be back in a minute,' he said. After ordering, he came back and placed the number on the table. 'I've bought us both a jam doughnut knowing how much you like them.'

She gave a shy smile, a hint of the old Ellie peeking through. 'I'm surprised you remembered.'

'Of course I did,' he said, his voice gentle and reassuring. He settled into his chair, ready to listen to whatever it was that had prompted this unexpected visit, determined to offer her the support and comfort she clearly needed.

Ever since Ellie had joined the police several years ago, he'd taken her under his wing. She was very shy and reserved until you got to know her, but what made her stand out from everyone else were her phenomenal research skills – something people didn't believe until they actually witnessed it. His old boss, Detective Chief Inspector Whitney Walker, had to fight tooth and nail to keep Ellie on the team because there was always someone trying to poach her. Luckily, Ellie enjoyed working with Whitney and the others and had never expressed any desire to move.

'Thanks, I skipped breakfast this morning,' Ellie said.

Matt didn't normally like to push people into talking, but knowing Ellie as he did, if he didn't broach the subject she'd sit there quietly stewing.

'Right, come on, tell me everything,' he said with empathy. 'I know there's something wrong. I'm all ears.'

'Is it that obvious?' she asked with a grimace.

'It is to me. Look... I don't want to force you into confiding in me if you'd rather not, but I hate seeing you like this.'

'Dean and I have finished,' Ellie said, tearfully.

'Oh no. When did this happen?'

'It was a few months ago but it's so hard to get over. The DCI knew and suggested I should take some time off and visit you. But then my granddad died, and so I had to stay to help my mum.' She sniffed and wiped her eyes with the back of her hand. 'It's like one thing after another. It's been such an awful time.'

'I'm so sorry, Ellie. I know how close you were to your granddad,' Matt said, reaching out and placing a friendly hand on her arm.

'He'd been ill for a while and in a way, it was a release. But it's still hard not to have him around.'

'I totally understand,' Matt said, his thoughts fleetingly

going back to when his wife, Leigh, was tragically killed in a road traffic accident. It still seemed like it was yesterday.

'You know, Granddad never did like Dean. He said there was something about him that he didn't trust and he warned me to be careful. At the time I put it down to him being over-protective of me. Because he was. But guess what... he was right. Dean had been cheating on me with someone from work.'

Matt's fists clenched, anger coursing through him for what that no-good boyfriend had done. The last time he'd spoken to Ellie, she'd sounded so happy and had been talking about them moving in together and heading to London when Dean had finished his nursing training because he wanted to work at one of the top London paediatric hospitals.

'What a bastard,' Matt muttered.

'You're not wrong. I thought I was getting over it, but then the other day, I was out with my friends in the pub, and he came in with her. They looked so happy... and in love.' She choked back a sob.

'You don't have to talk about it now if you don't want to,' Matt said softly, 'I can see how much it's upsetting you.'

'I do want to. It's the only way I'm going to get over it. Except there's nothing more to tell you. Oh – apart from he's also left me with a car loan to pay off.'

Matt scowled. 'Did you buy it between you?'

'No. The car's in my name but he was going to pay half. I can't even sell it yet because I wouldn't make enough money to cover what's left owing.'

'How are you managing?'

'I can just about cover my basic expenses, but it does mean no going out or new clothes for the next three years. Or at least until I get a pay rise.' Her shoulders slumped.

'How could you afford to come here?' Matt asked, guilt coursing through him that he wasn't able to offer any accommodation.

'My mum and dad paid for me. They knew how upset I was and thought it would do me good. Anyway, it doesn't matter. I'm glad to come down here for a break. And by the way, the others all send their love.'

He chuckled at the thought of Frank and Doug, two of the longstanding detective constables, *sending their love*.

'What's been happening in Lenchester recently?' he asked, looking forward to hearing news of the old place.

'Same old, same old. We're still like a magnet for murders, although you seem to be getting your fair share as well down here since you moved in.' Ellie grinned, the tension easing.

'Don't you start. My new team are saying that it's all my fault. They think I've brought the "Lenchester murder vibe" with me.' He did quote marks with his fingers.

'Well, that's ridiculous. You can't control how many murders there are.'

'That's what I keep saying. But it's only said in fun. It's a very different pace of life down here, though. Much slower. Which is good but can be frustrating. I used to take for granted the speedy response from forensics and other departments. Not now. But it's a great team and you'd definitely like them.' Matt chuckled to himself while thinking about the two teams. Both very different in some ways, but in others almost identical.

'What's your boss like?'

'Lauren. I mean, DI Pengelly? Hmm. Well, let's put it this way... she's certainly very different from Whitney, but just as driven, in a different way. And... she's... well let's say she can be spikey and unyielding, always wanting things her way. Although she does seem to be mellowing a bit, thank goodness.'

'Is that down to you?' Ellie asked, tilting her head to one side.

'Maybe a little,' Matt said with a small shrug. 'The main thing is, I really enjoy it down here. That doesn't mean I don't miss everyone in Lenchester, because I do. But it's working out well for Dani and me.'

'How's she doing?' Ellie asked, sounding concerned.

'She's great.' He paused a moment and let out a sigh. 'It's been ten months now since Leigh died, and Dani doesn't even mention her much now. We have photos up, and she'll sometimes talk about her, but that's it. She never asks when Leigh's coming back. At her age it's to be expected, I suppose. But it's still sad...' His words petered out.

'What about your mum and dad? How are they?' Ellie asked, bringing him out of his reverie.

'They've been amazing. I don't know what I'd do without them. I must admit it's very cramped where we live, but I need their support and plan to stay there for now.'

'Yes, of course. That's understandable.'

'I could have employed a full-time nanny and lived somewhere else... Maybe one day – but not yet.'

'You'll know when the time is right,' Ellie said, pausing while the waiter brought over the coffees and doughnuts.

'Thank you,' Matt said, laughing at the way Ellie's face suddenly brightened.

'This is such a treat,' Ellie said, picking up the doughnut and taking a bite, leaving sugar all around her lips. 'I think I've definitely made the right decision coming down here for a visit.'

'I'm sure you have,' Matt said. 'Anyway, what do you want to do today?' He glanced at his watch. 'We've got all day. We can go for a walk, go down to the beach. What do you fancy doing?'

'I'd like to see Dani again. When can we do that?'

'She's desperate to see you, too. But I said I didn't know our plans. She's at home with Mum and Dad. Why don't we finish up here and go back there. Maybe we could all go for a walk in the park?' His phone rang, and he glanced down at the screen that was on the table. 'Oh no.'

'What is it?' Ellie frowned.

'It's the DI. If she's phoning on my day off it's not good. I've got to get this. Sorry.' He answered the phone. 'Morning, ma'am.'

'Matt. I'm so sorry to call you when you're not on duty, but a woman's body has been found at an old farm near Penzance.'

'Do we know the circumstances?' Like he needed to ask.

'Unfortunately, it's most definitely murder. You'd better prepare yourself. I haven't been to the scene, but from what I gather, it's not a pretty sight.'

Everyone he worked with knew that he had an aversion to anything bloody or gory. He forced himself to face these things but it never got easier.

'Okay, ma'am. I'll meet you there,' he said, trying to hide his disappointment at being disturbed but not sure if he'd succeeded.

'I'm sorry, have I interrupted your plans? Were you going somewhere with the family?'

'Actually, I'm with an old colleague from Lenchester who's visiting for a couple of weeks, but I'm sure she'll understand.'

He heard Lauren suck in a breath. Was it because he'd mentioned his old place of work? She had a thing about him always comparing the two.

'Okay, meet me at the farm. I'll text you the details,' she said sharply.

'Thanks, ma'am.' He ended the call and sighed. 'I'm so sorry, Ellie. You'll never believe this, but it's a murder, and the DI wants me at the scene.'

'It's fine, don't worry,' Ellie said, giving an encouraging nod. 'I'm going to enjoy myself wandering around and taking in the quaint shops and stunning scenery.'

'I'll be in touch as soon as I can and will definitely see you later. Promise.'

'Don't worry on my account,' Ellie said with a flick of her hand. 'Work has to come first. You wouldn't be you if it didn't.'

He quickly finished his doughnut, took a few sips of coffee which was too hot to fully drink, and left.

'Bloody typical,' he muttered as he headed towards his car. 'Of all times for a murder to happen, it had to be now.'

TWO

SUNDAY, 14 JULY

Lauren pulled up outside the small farm on one of the back roads in Buryas Bridge. The farmhouse was a small, stone building with a thatched roof. A gravel path connected the main road to the house, with hedges and wildflowers on either side.

The area around the farm had green fields separated by hedges, with sheep grazing in some of them. Hills could be seen in the distance, partially obscured by the morning mist. A stream ran to the side of the property, making a soft sound as it flowed. Despite the idyllic setting, an unsettling stillness hung in the air. The usual sounds of farm life were conspicuously absent, replaced by an eerie silence broken only by the occasional chirping of birds and the soft rustling of leaves in the wind.

Lauren hurried over to the police officer who was standing on duty, her uniform standing out against the rural backdrop. The officer's solemn expression and the presence of the cordon near the barn hinted at the grim discovery that had shattered the peace of this quiet corner of the countryside.

'Morning, Constable. Where's the body?' she asked PC Amy Smith.

'In the barn, ma'am,' the officer said, pointing to the cordon.

'Has the pathologist arrived yet?' Lauren asked.

'No. There's only me and PC Hooper here.'

'Who found the body?' she asked, curious because there was no one standing close by.

'Mrs Carter, one of the woman's neighbours. It seems she called with some milk that the victim had asked her to buy, and there was no answer. She was concerned, looked round, went into the barn, and found her.'

'Do you have a name for the victim?'

'Yes, she's Carmel Driscoll.'

'Thanks. I'll interview Mrs Carter, shortly. Where is she?'

'Sitting in the car with Phil. I mean PC Hooper. She's in shock.'

The sound of another car drawing up distracted Lauren and she glanced in its direction. Matt had arrived.

'Thanks, Amy,' she said, turning back to the officer. 'I'll grab my sergeant, and then we'll have a look round the barn.'

'Okay, ma'am. Brace yourself. It's not very nice,' the officer said with a grimace. 'I nearly threw up all my breakfast when I went in there.'

'Yes, so I've heard,' Lauren said as she turned and headed over to where Matt had parked.

'Morning, ma'am,' Matt said as he got out of his car, appearing tense. No doubt because he wasn't looking forward to seeing the body.

'Hello, Matt. I'm sorry to impose on your day off. Were you doing anything special?'

'I was in a café in Penzance with Ellie, the ex-colleague I mentioned. She's here for a couple of weeks on holiday and understood why I had to leave.'

'Well, I'm sorry anyway. Our victim's Carmel Driscoll. The

woman who discovered the body is in the police car with one of the officers. Let's take a look in the barn while we wait for the pathologist.'

'Okay, ma'am,' Matt said, his jaw set.

'I know you're not going to like this, so why don't you walk behind me?' Lauren said kindly, trying to ease the pressure.

'I'll be fine, thanks, ma'am. And before you ask, no, I still haven't seen about having some hypnotherapy sessions. I know we have this conversation every time we see a body, but there never seems to be enough time in the day to sort it out.'

Lauren strode ahead with Matt slightly behind, and they walked into the barn. The pungent odour of death assaulted her nostrils as they approached the scene. The victim's lifeless body was in a sitting position on the floor propped up against some hay bales. Her arms were outstretched, twisted at unnatural angles, and her eyes stared vacantly ahead. It was like they'd been frozen in a final moment of terror.

Dried blood had pooled around her chest, the dark crimson stain contrasting sharply with her pale, lifeless skin. What appeared to be the fatal wound was a dark cavernous hole and the edges of the torn flesh were crusted with blackened blood.

Beside the body, a blood-encrusted knife protruded from the ground, a reminder of the life it had extinguished. The sight was enough to turn even the strongest stomach, and Lauren felt a wave of nausea wash over her as she took in the macabre display.

'My goodness,' she said, her voice quivering as she stared down at the knife, which was pinning down a note, the paper stained and partially obscured by the congealed blood.

Matt took a step forward next to her, his face pale. 'The killer has left us a message,' he said, his voice barely above a whisper. *'Ten green bottles.'*

The words on the note seemed to mock them, a twisted game left behind by a depraved mind.

'What's that meant to mean?'

'All I can think of is the children's counting song,' Lauren said with a shrug.

'Yes, you're right. We sing it to Dani. But why put it next to the body? Surely it doesn't mean...' His voice faltered. 'No, I won't say anything.'

Lauren arched an eyebrow, realising that Matt was thinking about the last murder case they'd dealt with when he proposed that they could be dealing with a potential serial killer.

'That's—'

'Good morning DI Pengelly, DS Price,' Henry's voice boomed out behind them, interrupting Lauren.

They turned around to greet the pathologist, who bumbled over towards them, carrying his old bag, which looked like it had been a constant companion since the pathologist first qualified at least thirty years ago. The leather exterior was heavily worn, with deep creases and scuff marks that spoke of countless crime scenes and postmortems.

'Good morning, Henry. We haven't touched anything. We've only been looking at the body and the surroundings,' Lauren clarified.

'No problem,' he said, taking a step forward. 'What have we got here?' He pulled out his camera and began snapping photos of the body. 'Ah, I see.'

'There's a note, pinned down by what we can assume to be the murder weapon,' Matt said.

'Never assume anything, my boy,' Henry said, lowering his camera and turning to Matt, a roguish glint in his eye. 'Because it makes an ass out of you and me.'

'Yes, I've heard that saying many times,' Matt said, chuckling in response.

'Having said that,' Henry added, his tone turning more serious, 'I suspect you're right and that it could be the murder weapon. From first glance, it looks like she was stabbed, the blade plunged deep into her chest. But I won't commit to that theory until she's at the morgue and I can conduct a thorough investigation. There might be more to this case than meets the eye. As so often happens.'

'Do you have any idea of how long she's been there?' Lauren asked.

'Well, judging by the state of rigor mortis and the pooling of the blood, I'd say she was killed sometime last night, between nine pm and four am but I'll give you a more precise time later,' Henry said.

'Okay, thanks, Henry. We're going to speak to the woman who found her. I'll wait to hear back from you.'

They left the barn and headed over to the police car. As they got there, the police officer got out of the back and so did an older woman who looked to be in her late sixties. Her face was pale, and there were red rings around her eyes. They walked over.

'Morning, ma'am,' the officer said. 'This is Mrs Carter who found the victim.'

'I'm very sorry for your loss,' Lauren said, turning to the woman. 'We do need to ask a few questions. Would you be up to that?'

'Yes,' Mrs Carter said quietly.

'Why don't we sit over there?' Lauren said, gesturing to the bench in the front garden of the victim's house. They headed over and sat down.

'Please, could you go through the events of this morning, up until when you found Carmel?' Lauren asked, staring intently at the witness.

The woman took a deep breath, her hands trembling. 'Yes, of course. Carmel asked me to buy her some milk when I went shopping yesterday. I only do a big shop every couple of weeks because the supermarket's quite far away. Carmel had already done hers, but she'd forgotten to buy milk. So, I got her some and brought it over this morning. I was out until late yesterday and didn't have time then.' She paused, tears welling as she continued, 'I knocked on the door, but there was no answer. It was slightly open, so I went inside and called her name. But she wasn't there.'

Lauren leant forwards, her brow furrowed. 'Is it unusual for the door to be left open?'

The woman shook her head. 'Yes. She's careful about security because of her ex-husband. He's a drunk and sometimes turns up asking for money.'

'I see,' Lauren said, making a mental note of the potential suspect. 'Please continue.'

The woman took a shuddering breath. 'And then, I walked into the barn, thinking that maybe she'd popped in there to see if the chickens had laid any eggs... and then I saw her...' Her voice faded into silence, and she gulped, visibly struggling to maintain her composure. 'It was awful. She was on the ground, so still and pale.'

Lauren reached out, placing a comforting hand on the woman's shoulder. 'What did you do then?' she asked softly.

'I stood for a few seconds in shock, unable to believe what I was seeing. Then, I ran out and phoned the police. My hands were shaking so badly I could barely press the numbers. They asked me to stay here until they arrived, which I did. I couldn't bear to go back inside, not with Carmel like that.' The woman's voice broke, and she buried her face in her hands.

'What can you tell us about Carmel?' Lauren asked after a few seconds.

Mrs Carter sat upright. 'She's a retired police officer, and since her divorce from Rhys, she's lived alone.'

Lauren grimaced. A murdered ex-cop was not what they needed.

'Do you know Rhys?'

'Yes. He's not a nice man and could be quite violent when

he'd been drinking. He didn't visit often, but sometimes I'd see his car parked outside the house.'

Lauren went on alert. Had the ex-husband paid her a visit and things got out of hand? It would make more sense than it being linked to her old job.

'Thank you very much for your help, Mrs Carter. We may need to speak to you again,' Lauren said, concluding the interview.

'Can I go home now?' Mrs Carter asked.

'Yes, of course. Would you like someone to take you?'

'No, I'll be fine, thanks. I only live over there,' she said, pointing about a hundred metres down the road to where there was another solitary house.

The woman left, and Lauren turned to Matt. 'We need to get onto this straight away. I hope it's nothing to do with her being an ex-officer but we can't discount it. Let's take a look in the house to see if there's been a disturbance.'

Inside everything appeared to be in order. The house was neat and tidy, with no signs of a struggle or forced entry.

'I'll check the kitchen to see if there's a knife missing,' Matt said, his voice tense as he left Lauren to investigate the lounge.

After a couple of minutes, he returned, the expression on his face unreadable.

'Well? What did you find?' Lauren asked, her heart racing.

'No knives appear to be missing,' Matt said. 'She has a knife block and it's full. There weren't any knives in any of the drawers. But I did find her laptop and phone on the table. Shall I bring them in for forensics to go through?' He pulled an evidence bag from his pocket.

'Yes, good idea.' Lauren nodded, her mind already racing with possibilities.

'I think she has a cat. There's a bowl of food with a little remaining and a scratching pole. But I haven't seen her.'

'If the door was open, she's probably gone outside. I'll ask officers to try and track it down. We also need to find the ex-husband and see what he was doing last night. I have a feeling he might be involved.'

'You think he's the killer?'

'It's too early to say for sure,' Lauren answered, her voice low and serious. 'But we need to explore every avenue. I'll see you back at the station.'

'Yes, ma'am,' Matt said, as he hurried out of the house, evidence bag in hand.

Lauren took one last look around the house. Her gut was telling her that this case would be a tough one to crack – but she was ready for the challenge.

THREE

SUNDAY, 14 JULY

Lauren drove back to the station, her mind racing with the tasks ahead. She parked, entered the building, and navigated the familiar hallways to her office. Dropping her bag with a thud on one of the chairs, she exhaled deeply, steadying herself for the day's challenges. With a brisk stride, she made her way to the room where the team was beginning to assemble. She had contacted Billy, ensuring his presence, while Clem and Jenna had been on duty and were already there. Tamsin was the only team member she hadn't been able to reach despite trying several times. She'd ended up leaving a message, but so far there'd been no response.

Approaching the whiteboard, Lauren waited for Matt, who'd arrived moments after her, to hang up his jacket, and take his place by her side.

'Good morning, everyone,' she started, her voice carrying an undercurrent of regret for the early intrusion. 'I'm sorry that those of you who weren't on duty had to come in. Which reminds me, does anyone know where Tamsin is? I've tried to call her several times and left a message but heard nothing.'

'I bet she's dead to the world,' Billy said with a laugh. 'She went out with friends last night and she intended to have a skinful.'

Lauren exhaled audibly, unable to hide her frustration. Although it wasn't the officer's fault. She had no idea that there'd be an emergency. 'Well, hopefully she'll call when she gets my message. We've got a nasty murder on our hands and everyone is needed.' She wrote the victim's name, *Carmel Driscoll*, on the board, and beneath it, linked the phrase *Ten Green Bottles* with an arrow.

'What's that about?' Billy's question cut through the silence.

'The victim was found with a knife wound to the chest and next to her, pinned to the ground with a knife, was a note with those words on it,' Lauren explained. 'I'll text you all the photo I took. The words were printed in a very fancy font on an A4 sheet of paper.'

'So it wasn't written?' Jenna asked. 'Does that make it more impersonal, do you think?'

'Not necessarily. All it means is that they don't want their handwriting to be analysed,' Clem said.

'Exactly,' Lauren confirmed, with a nod.

'"Ten Green Bottles" is a children's song, isn't it? I remember singing it at school,' Billy mused, his comment sparking a flicker of shared recollection among the team.

'Yes, that's right,' Lauren acknowledged. 'Carmel Driscoll was an ex-police officer. I'm not sure which station, but we need to start checking into her background and—'

The sudden ring of the phone on the desk next to where Lauren stood interrupted her. She swiftly moved to grab hold of the handset.

'Pengelly.'

'Morning, ma'am. It's Tamsin. I didn't realise you'd be answering. I thought one of the team would,' came the raspy voice from the other end, immediately drawing Lauren's full attention, as well as ruffling her feathers somewhat that the officer hadn't intended to speak directly to her but hoped to reach her colleagues.

'You don't sound well, is there anything wrong?' Lauren asked, not wanting to accuse the officer of being hungover. She did only have Billy's word for it.

'Not sick exactly, ma'am, but I am at the hospital.'

Lauren's mouth dropped open. 'What's happened? Are you okay?'

'Well, you're never going to believe this,' Tamsin began, her voice wavering slightly as if still in disbelief at her own tale. 'I went out skateboarding with my friends last night. It was a bit of fun, you know? I admit, we'd been drinking, which might have been a factor. I was at the skateboard park trying to do an ollie when—'

'A what?' Lauren interrupted.

'It's a trick where you bring the skateboard up into the air. Anyway, it didn't work out. I'm not sure but I might have twisted my body before jumping which sent me off balance. I took a pretty nasty fall and broke my leg.'

'If you broke your leg yesterday, why are you still at the hospital?' Lauren queried, a frown creasing her forehead.

'That's the trouble, ma'am. I'm going to be out of action for quite a while because I've got to have surgery,' Tamsin explained with a sigh. 'They said I need some pins in there – it's broken quite severely in a couple of places. I've seen on my mobile that you were trying to reach me while I was with the doctors. Is there a problem?'

Lauren's hand tightened around the phone. 'We've got a murder case on our hands—'

'What? Crap. There's no way I'm going to be able to help. I'm so sorry. I might be able to do something from my hospital bed and...' Her sentence hung unfinished in the air.

'No, of course you can't. I don't want you to worry, we'll

manage,' she said, trying to sound reassuring but her mind working overtime regarding how they were going to cope.

'Thanks, ma'am. Maybe Billy can help on the research, he's great at that.'

They also needed him for the investigation. Murders took up everyone's time.

'I'll sort something out. You concentrate on getting better. Let me know how it all goes.'

'Thanks, ma'am. I really am sorry and— Oh they've come to take me to the operating theatre. I've never had an operation before...'

'You'll be fine,' Lauren said, keeping her voice calm. 'Promise to keep in touch and let us know how you are.'

Lauren ended the call and sucked in a long breath. This couldn't have happened at a worse time.

She glanced at the rest of the team who were staring at her with open mouths, worry etched on their faces.

'What's happened to Tamsin, ma'am?' Billy asked, panic shining from his eyes. 'Is she okay?'

Billy was very close to Tamsin and it didn't surprise Lauren that he'd been the first to speak.

'Yes, I believe so. She's broken her leg and needs surgery. I'm not sure how long she's going to be off work.'

'How did she do that?' Billy asked.

'A skateboarding accident, after too much to drink.'

'Typical. Only Tamsin could do that,' Billy said, the corners of his mouth turning up in amusement. 'You wait until she's back at work. I'll give her a hard time. She's always saying how good she is at skateboarding. Clearly not as good as she thought.'

'Yes, well, it couldn't have happened at a worse time,' Lauren added, wanting to bring that conversation to an end. 'It's all hands on deck when we have a murder and she'll be missed because we need someone who can research into the victim and her life.'

'I can do that,' Billy said, frowning. 'You know that, ma'am. I'm as good as Tamsin.'

'Then who will do your allocated tasks? We need CCTV analysing, interviews with neighbours, friends, social media checks etc. etc... You know the drill.'

Maybe she should request help from another station – but that would mean taking time out to ensure they were able to follow her instructions and that would slow everything.

'Ma'am, can I have a word?' Matt said quietly, cutting across her thoughts.

He beckoned her over to beside the board where they were out of earshot.

'What is it?'

'Remember I said that my friend and ex-colleague, Detective Constable Ellie Naylor, is staying here for a couple of weeks? Why don't we ask her to come in and help us? She's amazing at research. It's her main responsibility in the Lenchester team.'

Lauren shook her head, not even contemplating his suggestion, which was totally impractical. 'No. Thanks for the offer, but there's no way it would work. She's not going to know the team or the area, for that matter. Quite frankly, I think it could be more trouble than it's worth. You of all people know what it's like when a new officer joins a team. It can take ages to get them up to speed.'

'I got thrown into a dead body case on the day I arrived, remember?'

'That's different. You're a sergeant and more experienced. As much as I'd like to say yes, it wouldn't work.'

'You're wrong, ma'am,' Matt said, standing his ground and looking directly at her. 'Ellie would be good. More than good. How about you meet her first, and then decide? You've got nothing to lose.'

'Except valuable time,' Lauren muttered, already thinking that she wasn't going to win this one.

'It won't take long. You can see for yourself how good she is. If you agree to use her, we could consider her a civilian worker tasked with sitting at the computer researching into aspects of the case. She can help us solve this. I'm sure of it. I wouldn't suggest her if I wasn't one hundred per cent certain she could help speed up the investigation.'

'I don't know... It's not really going to help...' She shifted from foot to foot.

'I promise, if you decide against using her, Ellie won't take offence. She's not like that.'

'Why haven't you mentioned her before?'

If she was that extraordinary, then surely he would have spoken about the officer before now.

'I don't know,' he said awkwardly.

'Well, tell me about her now.'

'Ellie's in her mid-twenties, quiet and unassuming. She's a conscientious and hard worker. She's also popular with her colleagues. I've never heard a bad word said against her. I know you think I'm biased... well, maybe I am... but we'd be lucky to have her, even if it's only for a couple of days.'

'You're very convincing, Matt,' she said with a resigned grin. 'Okay, ask her in for a chat. But no promises. If I think it won't work then I'll say so.'

'Good call, ma'am,' Matt said, with a sharp nod. 'You won't regret it. I'll contact Ellie and ask if she'll come in for a chat. Hopefully, she agrees after all my persuading.'

FOUR
SUNDAY, 14 JULY

Matt went down to the entrance of the station and into the car park to wait for Ellie, who was driving in. It had taken him a while to persuade her, and she finally agreed to come in after he explained that if she really didn't want to help once she'd met the DI and the others, then it would be fine to say no.

After a few minutes she appeared driving a metallic red Volkswagen Polo. Was that the car Dean had persuaded her to buy? He hurried over to where she'd parked.

'The roads are so winding around here,' Ellie said as she scrambled out of the car, her hands fidgeting with her car keys. 'Thank goodness I drive a Polo because otherwise I wouldn't have made it along some of the roads. And even then, I closed my eyes several times when trying to squeeze between two cars. Actually, you didn't hear that from me.'

Matt laughed. 'I agree it can be scary but you'll soon get used to it. You can always tell the locals from the visitors because they know the roads and nip in and out all of the time.'

'I'll take your word for it. You know, I'm still worried about doing this. Are you really sure you need my help?' She chewed down on her bottom lip.

'Look, Ellie, we're a small team as it is, and now Tamsin's off work with a broken leg it's not good. And she really is the one who's best at the research. Billy's good, too, but we need him out in the field. Even if you can help for today to get us started, that would be a great help.'

'Well, I don't want to be treading on anyone's toes.' Ellie shifted from one foot to the other, her shoulders hunched slightly.

'Where's the harm? You're on holiday, and Tamsin's not here. I've already told you that they're a good bunch. You'll find they'll be very supportive. We need something to get us going on the case. You know what it's like when we first have a murder. As much information as we can get, as soon as possible, is going to help. Time is of the essence. And,' he added a thought suddenly entering his head, 'you'll be paid for helping – you mentioned being strapped for cash.'

'I could certainly do with some money... You won't leave me on my own, will you?' Ellie's voice wavered slightly, and she wrapped her arms around herself.

Matt turned to her. It was like she'd gone back to when she first started at Lenchester. But he guessed she'd been through a lot recently, so he couldn't hold it against her.

'It will be fine, so don't worry. Come with me,' he said kindly.

As they entered the office, the usual buzz of conversation instantly ceased as everyone turned to focus on them.

Damn. That wasn't what he wanted.

They headed over to Lauren, who was standing by the board on the phone. Her call ended a few seconds after they reached her.

'Ma'am, this is Ellie. She's agreed to give us a hand if you'd like her to,' Matt said, gesturing with his hand to his friend.

'Good morning, Ellie. It's kind of you to assist although, to be honest, I do have my reservations as to how much you can do, considering you're new to the area and don't know me or the team.'

'I realise that, guv, but—'

'It's ma'am,' Matt said quietly, interrupting Ellie.

'Oh. Sorry, ma'am. But if you do need some extra help, then I'm willing to step in for today.' Ellie glanced at Matt, who gave an encouraging nod.

Lauren's lips pressed into a thin line. 'I'm not entirely convinced this is the best course of action,' she said, doubt in her voice. 'But I suppose we're short-staffed, and if Matt vouches for you, we can give it a try. But don't expect to be privy to all the details of the case right away.'

She gestured towards a desk in the corner. 'Why don't you sit over there, at Tamsin's desk? It's next to Billy. Find out what you can about Carmel Driscoll. She's our victim. All we know so far is that she's an ex-police officer. We're not sure from which force. She's divorced and has a violent ex-husband, according to the neighbour.'

'Yes, ma'am,' Ellie said, quietly.

'I'll set you up on the computer,' Matt said. As they walked over, an uncomfortable silence hung between them. 'Let me introduce you to the team,' he said, conscious of their every move being scrutinised by the team. 'This is Billy.' He nodded at the officer.

'Hello,' Billy said gruffly.

Matt frowned in his direction, a wordless reprimand. He was meant to be nice to Ellie. She was there to help them.

'Hi, Ellie,' Jenna said, warmly. 'Thanks for coming in to help. Ignore grumpy pants over there, he's been like this since his girlfriend dumped him last week.' She rolled her eyes in Billy's direction.

'No I haven't. I'm over it now, anyway. I'm worried about Tamsin, that's all.'

'We all are,' Matt said, grateful for Jenna being welcoming.

'That's Jenna and next to her is Clem. And that's it. We're a small team.'

'Hello,' Ellie said, her hands fidgeting at her sides.

'Right, let me sign you in, and I'll leave you to it...' Matt said.

'Okay,' she said, settling into the chair at the computer, her shoulders hunched.

Matt left her and headed back to his desk. His jaw clenched, on the way, he nodded for Billy to join him.

'What is it, Sarge?' Billy asked, a smirk playing at the corners of his mouth. Clearly the officer knew why he was being called over.

'Billy,' Matt said quietly, his voice strained, 'I know we're going to miss Tamsin, but there's no need for you to have that attitude with Ellie. She's here to help.'

'But Sarge... I don't want her taking Tamsin's place, that's all. Tamsin's good at her job,' Billy said, avoiding Matt's glare.

'Yes, I know that, but so is Ellie, and you'll see there's no one who can research like her. Teams at Lenchester are falling over backwards trying to steal her from my old boss, DCI Walker. But Ellie won't move. She is one of the team. So, there's no need for you to worry. She won't be staying here. Give her a chance, okay?' Matt's words came out in a rush, his frustration evident.

'Sorry, I didn't mean to be mean. I was worried about how things would go, that's all.' Billy's apology sounded half-hearted, but Matt wasn't going to pursue it.

'Why don't you give Tamsin a call later and see how she's doing. I'm sure she'll appreciate it.'

'Yes, I suppose I could.'

'Make sure to tell her that we all wish her better and—'

'Matt,' Ellie called out, her voice filled with excitement. 'I mean, Sarge.'

'It's Matt. I don't need to be called anything else,' Matt said, leaving Billy and rushing over to her, his eyebrows raised in anticipation. 'Have you got something?'

'Yes. Quite a bit, actually.'

Matt chuckled to himself. That was even quicker than he'd anticipated.

'Okay, I'll fetch the DI.'

He practically sprinted to Lauren's office and tapped on the door, his heart pounding with excitement. He could see through the glass that Lauren hadn't even had time to sit down.

'What is it?' she said, as he burst in.

'Ellie's feeding back and I assumed you'd want to hear it.'

'Already?' Lauren's eyes widened in disbelief. 'I've only just left the room.'

They hurried back and stood beside Ellie. The rest of the team were also listening.

'Okay, Ellie, let's hear it,' Matt said, leaning forward eagerly.

'Yes, Sarge. Carmel Driscoll worked for the Devon & Cornwall force for the whole of her policing career. She was mainly at Camborne, where she was born. She was married to another officer, his name is Rhys, but he was fired from the police force for being drunk on duty in 2004. This was after a number of warnings. She has a pension from the police and also another small private pension. Her state pension doesn't kick in yet because she isn't old enough. She's been living in Buryas Bridge for ten years. She divorced her husband three years ago. I haven't yet checked her social media, but I thought this might be a useful starting point for you.' Ellie glanced up at Matt, her cheeks tinged pink.

Matt looked over at Lauren, who appeared stunned, pride swelling in his chest.

'Well, that's... that's bloody brilliant,' Billy said, his voice filled with awe, breaking the silence.

Matt shot him a grateful look. Clearly Billy was trying to make up for his behaviour before and it was appreciated.

'I agree with Billy. That's absolutely incredible,' Lauren said, shaking her head in amazement. 'And I'm sorry I doubted your ability, Ellie. If you'd be prepared to help us while Tamsin's off, we'd be extremely grateful, wouldn't we?' She looked at each of the team in succession, who were all nodding vigorously, their faces a mix of shock and admiration.

Matt had to bite back a laugh at Lauren's sudden change of heart, not to mention how surprised he was at her asking the team's opinion.

'I'm here for two weeks on holiday...' Ellie said. 'I'll do whatever I can to help, if you'd like me to.'

'You can't spend your whole holiday here with us,' Clem said, frowning. 'There are so many sights to see. Is this your first visit to Cornwall?'

'Yes,' Ellie said, colouring slightly.

'I can recommend lots of areas to visit. For a start there's—'

'Enough with the sightseeing tips, Clem,' Lauren snapped, her voice sharp. 'We have work to do.'

Matt caught sight of Billy and Jenna exchanging a knowing glance, their lips quirked. Just when he thought the DI had settled into an easy relationship with the team, she came out with a comment reminiscent of how she used to be in the past.

'Um... okay, sorry, ma'am,' Clem said, sheepishly.

'But I'm sure Ellie would be glad of some advice at another time,' Matt said, wanting to defuse the situation. 'It's always nice to have a local's perspective when visiting a new place.'

Lauren glanced at Matt, her expression softening slightly. 'That's a good idea. Now, Ellie, are you happy to help us? You'll be paid by the hour.'

'Yes, ma'am. I can stay as long as you need me – and I guess it would be nice to get out as well to visit places.' Ellie's face lit up, her excitement evident at the prospect of exploring Cornwall.

'I understand. Remember to keep an hourly timesheet of the work you do. Now, I don't suppose you had time to discover more about the husband, did you?' Lauren said, her attention back on the case.

'Actually, yes, ma'am, I did. I forgot to say, he lives on Queensway in Hayle, which is eight miles from here... Um... of course you know that,' Ellie muttered, her cheeks flushing. 'I've downloaded a photo of him, which I can forward to Matt, I mean, Sarge.'

'That's excellent. Thank you very much, Ellie. Right, let's get cracking. I want CCTV footage checked as close to the victim's house as we can, and people coming in and out late at night from Penzance and other areas. Sergeant Price and I are going to visit the ex-husband. Ellie, if you need any help with anything, ask one of the team.'

'Thanks, ma'am,' Ellie said gratefully.

'We're really glad to have you here, Ellie,' Jenna said sincerely.

'Absolutely,' Billy chimed in. 'With your skills, we'll crack this case in no time.'

Matt took a step towards her, his own smile wide. 'Thanks, Ellie. We appreciate this more than you know.'

FIVE

SUNDAY, 14 JULY

Matt stared out of the window on their way to Hayle, admiring the rugged coastline in the distance and the way the sun cast golden hues over the fields and ancient stone walls that segmented them.

'Well, you weren't wrong when you said how extraordinary Ellie is,' Lauren said, her hands firmly on the wheel.

She tossed a glance in his direction, before focusing back on the road.

'You have to see Ellie to realise what she's capable of. It's impossible to describe accurately,' Matt said, a hint of pride in his voice.

He leant back, watching the scenery blur past, remembering times in the past when people had been dumbstruck by Ellie's amazing talent. How someone so young could possess such a rare gift was totally beyond him. And what made it even more incredible was that she was so self-effacing when it came to her talent. It was as if she took it for granted and didn't value it in the same way others did.

'Is she a hacker?' Lauren asked.

He glanced at her, noticing a worried expression crossing her face as she navigated a sharp bend.

Lauren wasn't the first person to ask that, and no doubt wouldn't be the last.

'Probably a better question to ask is: does Ellie use her skills ethically? In which case, I can categorically answer yes. I'd class her as an ethical hacker and she uses her talent to help us solve cases. But to be honest, it's not something we've ever discussed openly because we accept that's how she is. Ellie has the ability to find information from various places and has a mine of knowledge about exactly where to go and the quickest way to access it. She's an incredible talent, that's for sure,' Matt explained.

'Maybe we should ask her to come and work for us full-time,' Lauren said, a grin playing at the corners of her mouth.

'I'm not sure that would work, ma'am. Especially as that would leave Tamsin superfluous to requirements.' Matt's gaze drifted to the passing countryside, contemplating the implications of pushing aside a member of the team.

'I was being flippant. Well, sort of. Tamsin's probably going to be off work for a couple of months and we'll certainly need someone to fill in.' She paused a moment, staring directly ahead at the road. 'You know, maybe Ellie could do a secondment down here. What do you think your DCI Walker would say about that?'

Matt glanced at her. Was she serious? Or joking? Or maybe testing the waters?

'DCI Walker would, of course, consider Ellie's request if it was what she wanted,' Matt answered, knowing that was the truth, but also realising it wouldn't be that easy. 'But I suspect she's not going to want to let Ellie go that easily... But anyway, this is all hypothetical,' he added, not wanting to dwell on something that could potentially cause issues from all sides. 'Let's get on with the case and see how much Ellie can help us in the two weeks that she's with us.'

Not to mention that Ellie might not want to stay any longer – nor would she be happy about her future being planned in her absence.

'You're right. I was getting carried away.' Lauren chuckled, her eyes crinkling at the corners as she reached up and tucked a stray strand of hair behind her ear.

'Right turn here, ma'am,' he added quickly, as Queensway was almost upon them.

Lauren turned and they drove along the road until they reached Driscoll's grey-rendered, mid-terraced house, with a rust-coloured front door. They walked up the short path and, using the door knocker, Matt banged loudly three times.

After waiting a couple of minutes, he knocked again, only this time even louder. As he did, the door to the neighbouring house opened, and a woman in her late sixties, with short silver hair framing her face, stood on her doorstep staring at them.

'You won't find him here, not at this time of day,' she said, glancing down at her watch, her lips pursed in suspicion.

'Where might we find Mr Driscoll?' Matt asked, taking a step towards the woman. 'Is he at work?'

'Work?' She gave a sarcastic laugh. 'I doubt it. You'll probably find him at the local pub. That's where he always is. He's a drinker.' She tutted in disapproval.

'I'm DCI Pengelly from Penzance police, and this is DS Price,' Lauren introduced, joining Matt close to the boundary between the two properties, which was marked only by a very low hedge. 'Would you mind answering a few questions?'

'Do you have ID?' the woman asked, staring directly at them.

'Yes,' Matt said, pulling out his warrant card from his pocket and showing the woman, while Lauren did the same.

'Thanks. You can't be too careful these days. You hear all

sorts of horror stories about people conning their way into some-one's house and then stealing their stuff. I'm Nancy Fry and I live here with my husband, Gordon. You can ask me anything. Would you like to come in? I've just put the kettle on.' The woman gestured towards the inside of her house.

'Thanks for the offer, Mrs Fry, but we don't have time,' Lauren said. 'This won't take long. We're interested in what Mr Driscoll has been doing over the last twenty-four hours. Did you see him at any time during this period?'

'Well,' Mrs Fry said, placing her hands squarely on her hips and shaking her head. 'Let me tell you about last night. He didn't get home until very late. As in the early hours of the morning, in fact. Probably around two, I reckon. Talk about thoughtless,' she growled, while at the same time rolling her eyes.

Clearly there was no love lost between the neighbours.

'How do you know the time he got back?' Matt asked.

'I'll give you three guesses,' the woman said, with a sigh. 'Because he woke me up with his banging and crashing,' she added without giving Matt a chance to reply. 'It was so loud it felt like he was in the room with us. You know, these houses are quite well insulated so they're not like some of those on the other side of town where you can hear your neighbours even when they're whispering. But Rhys is so loud that it doesn't make a difference and—'

'Does he often come in late and wake you?' Matt asked, interrupting the woman, and stopping her from going off on a tangent because they really needed to get on.

'Hmmm. I don't want you to think that I moan all the time, but it's not unusual on a Saturday night for him to come home plastered and cause a commotion. Either he can't get his key in the lock, or once inside, he falls over something. I'm telling you, if you decide to live in a terraced house like this, check who your neighbours are first. Mind you, that wouldn't have worked here because we moved in years before him, but you know what I mean.'

'Does Mr Driscoll live on his own?' Lauren asked.

'Yes. But he does have women staying with him sometimes. Not that I'm a nosey neighbour or anything,' Mrs Fry replied, colouring slightly.

'Is he with the same woman every time?' Matt asked. If Driscoll had a regular partner, they would attempt to question her.

'Ummm... not really, although recently I've seen the same woman more than once. She's been here maybe two or three times. But there are other women as well in between her visits,' Mrs Fry said, clearly disapproving.

'Do you know the name of this woman?' Matt asked.

'No. Of course not. I don't spend my time spying on Rhys. I'm just telling you what I've noticed.'

'Of course, and we're grateful for your information,' Matt said, wanting to placate the woman. 'How well do you know Rhys?' he added.

'We're neighbours, that's all. If we bump into each other on the doorstep we'll speak. You know, say hello and stuff.'

'Have you ever complained to him about his behaviour when he's been drinking?'

'Are you kidding me? He's not the sort of man you approach. I don't want to talk ill of him, but he's quite rough. He did have a go at my Gordon once. He said Gordon had taken up too much space when he parked and that stopped him from being able to park outside his house,' Mrs Fry recounted, a frown creasing her forehead as she recalled the incident.

'Did he hurt him?' Matt's voice grew more intense.

'No. He didn't actually hit Gordon, but he made it clear that if he did it again, there'd be trouble,' she admitted, her hands twisting together as she spoke, betraying her nervousness about revealing too much. 'My Gordon would never say "boo" to a goose, so I don't know why he had to be so mean,' she added quickly, as if trying to downplay the seriousness of the encounter. 'Maybe Rhys was drunk at the time. I don't know. He does seem to be angrier when he is, that's for sure.'

'Do you know whether Mr Driscoll works?' Matt asked, keen to move the questioning on.

'I think he does security work but it doesn't seem to be regular.'

'How do you know?' Matt asked.

'Because he works at all different times. Sometimes he doesn't work for days and then he might be out for two or three days, or nights, on the trot.'

'How do you know he's going to work at these times?' Lauren asked.

'Because of what he's wearing. For work he's always dressed in black jeans and black T-shirt. Other times he's dressed in more scruffy clothes.'

Matt bit back a grin. For someone who wasn't a nosey neighbour, she certainly had provided them with a lot of information.

'Could Mr Driscoll be working today?' Lauren asked, repeating the question Matt had asked the woman earlier. 'Did you see him go out?'

'No, I didn't see him leave, so I suppose he could be working. But I'd check the pub first if you're looking for him. Why do you want to speak to him anyway? What's he done?'

'Nothing for you to be concerned over. We're here to question him regarding one of our inquiries,' Lauren reassured her.

'Good. We don't want any trouble round here. It's a nice neighbourhood...' Her voice trailed off as she glanced at Driscoll's front door. 'Well, mainly it is. Anyway, like I said you'll probably find him at the local pub so try there first. Go to the top of the road, turn left, and it's at the bottom of the street.

It's called the Bear and Hound. You can't miss it.' She pointed down the road.

'Thank you for your time,' Matt said, smiling. 'We appreciate your help.'

'It's my pleasure,' Mrs Fry said. 'If I do see him later, shall I say you're looking for him? In case you haven't found him.'

'No, thanks. I'd rather you keep our conversation to yourself,' Lauren said, her voice firm.

'Okay. I get it.' Mrs Fry clamped her mouth shut and nodded.

As they left, Matt glanced over his shoulder, noting that Mrs Fry was still staring at them. He refrained from speaking until they were back in the car and out of earshot.

'Well, that confirms what Carmel Driscoll's neighbour has already told us about the ex-husband. He drinks and can be violent,' he said, glancing at Lauren.

'Yes,' Lauren agreed, her lips pressed together into a thin line. 'Let's go to the pub and see what he has to say for himself. Assuming that's where he is, of course.'

Matt nodded. The encounter with the neighbour had provided valuable insight into Driscoll, but now it was time to hear the man's side of the story.

SIX

SUNDAY, 14 JULY

Lauren drove to the pub, the anticipation knotted in her stomach. On the way, she took a sideways glance at Matt. She appreciated the fact that he'd offered Ellie to come and help them and briefly wondered about the nature of their friendship. Was there anything between them? She was a lot younger than him – not that age made any difference. But Matt still seemed wedded to the memory of his dead wife, Leigh. Anytime he mentioned Leigh, which wasn't often, the love he had for her shone out. Lauren suspected that Matt and Ellie were good friends and nothing more. Not that it was any of her business. And she would never dream of asking. She was, perhaps, a little curious about their relationship, though.

They drove into the pub car park, which was full. The Bear and Hound was clearly a popular spot. Not that Lauren had visited it before. As they entered through the white door, the noise and the smell of beer enveloped them. The pub was alive with chatter and laughter, and the atmosphere thick with the warmth of dim, flickering lights. A cheer went up towards the back of the pub where two couples were playing darts. Had one of them scored a bullseye? Or whatever it was. Lauren had never played the game.

'He's over there, ma'am,' Matt said, distracting her and tilting his head towards the bar.

Lauren's eyes followed, landing on the man from the photo that Ellie had sent them. Rhys Driscoll sat hunched over the bar, his grizzled features set in a scowl. They headed over to where he was perched, nursing a pint of beer. His fingernails were short and bore the stains of nicotine. The golden hue of the amber liquid in his glass was at odds with the rest of him.

'Mr Driscoll?' Lauren asked, raising her voice to be heard over the din of conversation and clinking glasses.

He turned slowly, taking a moment to focus on them. 'Who's asking?'

'I'm Detective Inspector Pengelly from Penzance CID, and this is Detective Sergeant Price. We'd like a word with you.'

Driscoll snorted. 'Yeah, I thought you were cops. I can spot you a mile off. And in answer to your question – if it was a question: I don't wish to speak to you. So piss off.'

Lauren glanced to the side, checking if anyone was eavesdropping. She noticed the woman behind the bar whose body language clearly showed she was listening, despite serving a customer.

'You're not curious as to what it's about?' Lauren pressed, her voice low but firm.

'I don't care. I've more important things to think about – like making sure to drink this pint before the beer gets too warm, and whether I'm going to watch the match this afternoon on telly,' Driscoll said, sounding nonchalant.

'Well, we're going to tell you anyway,' Lauren said, refusing to take his bait. She could feel the eyes of the other patrons on them, curious glances thrown their way as the locals picked up on the tension.

'Suit yourself,' Driscoll said, his indifference hanging in the air between them like a challenge.

Lauren took a breath, preparing herself. 'I'm very sorry to tell you that your wife, Carmel, has been killed.' She observed, with interest, the man's reaction to the news.

'You mean ex-wife,' he said, his face displaying no emotion whatsoever. He took another swig of his beer.

'Yes, your ex-wife,' Lauren confirmed, continuing to watch him closely for any crack in his composure.

'Accident, was it?' he asked in a nonchalant tone.

'No. I'm sorry to tell you that she was murdered.'

'Murdered... Carmel? Well, there's a turnup for the books.' He gave a hollow laugh and around them, conversations faltered as people strained to hear, clearly eager for a bit of juicy gossip.

'What's that meant to mean?' Matt asked, frowning.

'Nothing... well... she was always so perfect, like butter wouldn't melt in her mouth. Always had to do the right thing – and look where it got her. It goes to show that being a do-gooder guarantees you nothing.'

'You don't seem at all bothered by your ex-wife's demise, Mr Driscoll,' Matt said, his tone edged with disbelief.

'How the hell do you know how *bothered* I am? Just because I'm not bursting into tears doesn't mean I'm not upset by it... Except... I suppose I don't really care. Why should I? She's my ex-wife and got all she could out of me. How I feel about it is nothing to do with you,' he snapped.

'Fine,' Matt said, waving a hand, as if he couldn't care less about Driscoll's response.

Lauren observed the exchange, internally admiring Matt's ability to appear cool and calm, despite his tense jaw giving away his true feelings to anyone who knew him well. Being able to hide his thoughts was a skill she valued, albeit one she found

herself struggling to emulate at times, especially now that they
were faced with Driscoll's callous indifference.

'Where were you last night, Mr Driscoll, between the hours
of eight and four in the morning?' Lauren asked, determined to
bring the conversation back on track.

'So now you're accusing me of murdering my ex-wife, are
you?' Driscoll snapped. He picked up his beer, took a large
swallow and continued drinking until the glass was empty.

'No one's accusing you of anything at this stage. We're
trying to establish your whereabouts as part of our investigation,' Lauren said evenly. 'You of all people should know the
process.'

'I don't care what you want. I'm not going to talk to you
other than to say that if my ex-wife was killed, it was nothing to
do with me. I get it, I'm an ex-cop and it's always easy to accuse
the husband, or ex-husband. It saves you having to look for the
truth. Now, if you don't mind, I'd like to get back to my drinking
because you're annoying me. Lizzie,' he called out. 'Get me
another.' He pushed the empty glass to the back of the bar as
the woman headed over.

Lauren leant forward, placing her arm in front of the glass
so it couldn't be taken. 'That won't be necessary, Mr Driscoll.
You'll be coming with us.' She glanced at Lizzie. 'You can
leave us.'

The woman didn't need telling twice and hurried away.

'You can't do that,' Driscoll said, his face reddening. 'I've
done nothing wrong.'

'We have every right to take you to the station for questioning, especially given your lack of cooperation,' Lauren stated
firmly. 'You've no one to blame but yourself. So, come on.'

'No way. You can forget that. I'm not going with you. You'll
have to force me.' He folded his arms tightly across his chest and
stared at them, his bloodshot eyes defiant.

Lauren groaned inwardly, her frustration reaching boiling

point, but she was determined to keep her voice calm and low. 'Mr Driscoll, I suggest you come outside with us now, and we'll wait for uniformed officers to take you to the station at Penzance. Failing that, I will arrest you in front of everyone here, including putting on the handcuffs. I'm sure you don't want that to happen.' Her tone made it clear that it wasn't a request.

Driscoll glared at her for a few seconds then seemed to deflate slightly. 'Fine, fine, whatever you say. Let's go,' he acquiesced, waving his hand. 'Hold that beer, Lizzie. I'll be back soon,' he shouted across the bar.

They escorted him through the pub and outside. Before the door had even closed behind him, they were able to hear the pub erupting into excited chatter. The patrons were no doubt already spreading the news of Carmel's murder and speculating about Driscoll's involvement. Lauren suspected it would be all over the area by morning. They'd have to move fast if they were to keep ahead of the rumour mill.

Once outside, Lauren called for a car to take him in for questioning, the fresh air a welcome relief after the stuffiness of the pub. The late morning sun cast a warm glow on the quiet street, a contrast to the tense atmosphere surrounding them.

'Why can't I go in your car?' Driscoll protested, his belligerence returning now that they were away from inquisitive stares. His face was flushed, and his hands clenched into fists at his sides.

'Because we're doing this the correct way, Mr Driscoll. And don't attempt to run because there's no way you'll escape from us,' Lauren warned him, her voice firm and unwavering.

She glanced to either side of them, taking in the narrow alleyways and the few pedestrians going about their business. It wouldn't be easy for him to make his escape, and she didn't actually believe he would because he'd be captured within minutes.

'I have no intention of doing that. My running days are over.' He gestured to his protruding stomach as if to emphasise the point, his lips twisting into a sneer. 'But I'm telling you, you're barking up the wrong tree if you think I had anything to do with that bitch's death because—'

'Save your excuses for when we're at the station,' Lauren said, cutting him off with a sharp wave of her hand. 'I don't want to hear another word from you until we're in the interview room.'

'Suit yourself,' Driscoll said, kicking the gravel from under his feet and scowling at Lauren and Matt. The pebbles scattered across the ground, the sound echoing in the quiet street. 'But you're wrong. And now wasting valuable time if you want to catch whoever it was that killed my ex.'

Lauren exchanged a look with Matt as they waited for the car to arrive, both of them silently acknowledging that this was going to be a long day. The tension hung heavy in the air between them, but Lauren's determination never wavered. She was resolute in her pursuit of the truth, no matter how uncooperative Driscoll might be.

The distant sound of an approaching car signalled that their journey to the station was about to begin. As the car pulled up and uniformed officers escorted Driscoll into the back seat, Lauren couldn't shake the feeling that this case was going to be more complicated than it first appeared. Driscoll's reaction, or rather lack thereof, to the news of Carmel's death was unsettling. She'd dealt with her fair share of grieving relatives over the years, and his response was far from typical. Then again, just because he had a grudge against his ex-wife didn't mean he was guilty of her murder.

She sighed and rubbed her temples, a sense of foreboding washing over her. This case was going to test her. Test the whole team, for that matter. Nothing about it was shaping up to be typical. A former police officer murdered in her own home and her ex-husband a prime suspect. But they had the note to consider. 'Ten Green Bottles' hinted that there were nine more murders to come. Except... what would be Driscoll's motivation for further killings?

The only thing she knew for certain was that this whole case had all the makings of becoming a media circus if they weren't careful.

SEVEN

SUNDAY, 14 JULY

As soon as Matt returned to the office, he made a beeline for Ellie, who was immersed in her work at Tamsin's desk, the laptop belonging to Carmel Driscoll open beside her. She appeared intently focused on the screen, her brow furrowed in concentration.

'Have you got anything?' he asked, causing Ellie to start. 'Sorry, I didn't mean to make you jump.'

'That's okay. I tried to contact someone in the forensics department, but there was no one there who could help. So, I've had a look myself, to see if I could get into the laptop. I hope that's okay,' Ellie said, chewing on her bottom lip.

'Of course it is. You do what you can, and if there are any issues to deal with, that's down to me to sort out,' Matt reassured her. He doubted anyone would kick up if it meant the investigation was progressed. 'So, what have you found? Don't keep me in suspense.'

'There's a series of emails sent over the last few weeks to Carmel Driscoll and—' Ellie began, as she navigated through the files.

'Hang on a minute,' Matt interjected, holding up his hand

to pause her. A thought had struck him. 'We need everyone else to hear this, including the DI. Put the emails onto the screen,' he suggested, pointing at the monitor on the wall. 'And I'll get the DI.'

He marched quickly to Lauren's office and knocked on the door, his heart racing with anticipation as he waited for his boss's response. This could be the break they needed in the case.

'Come in,' she called out.

'Ma'am, Ellie's found some relevant emails on Carmel Driscoll's laptop which I assumed you'd want to see.'

'Great,' Lauren said, pushing back her chair, and walking with him into the office where an inbox was on the screen showing a list of emails.

Matt's eyes darted across the screen, trying to absorb as much information as possible.

'Are these the victim's emails?' Billy asked.

'Ellie, please explain,' Lauren said.

'Yes, this is the victim's inbox which I've gone through,' Ellie said, after clearing her throat. 'For each of the last four weeks the victim was sent an identical email. I'll open one of them for you to see. It warns her to watch her back.'

On the screen appeared one of the emails.

Matt's brows pulled together. Who was sending these threats?

'And how did you manage to find these?' Lauren enquired, her gaze shifting between Ellie and the screen.

'Because forensics were busy, I managed to open the laptop myself. I hope that's okay, ma'am?' Ellie asked, a hint of apprehension in her voice.

Matt held his breath, hoping that the DI wouldn't question Ellie's methods.

'Of course it is,' Lauren said. 'Can you trace who sent the emails?'

'Unfortunately not. They've used an IP address that can't be traced. I expect they've used what's known as a Tor network,' Ellie responded, her tone turning sombre.

'Oh, I think I've heard of that,' Clem chimed in, sounding eager to contribute.

'We forgot to mention, Ellie, that Clem's nickname is Clemipedia because he knows everything,' Billy said.

'Not everything, thank you, Billy,' Clem said modestly. 'But I do know about this. It's how an email can be sent without the IP address being traced. I'm not exactly sure how it works, though.'

'Yes,' Ellie said. 'The Tor network is free software that anyone can download, which enables someone to communicate anonymously. It routes the Internet traffic through multiple layers of servers and, in the end, it's virtually impossible to trace where it came from.'

'Do a lot of people use this network?' Matt asked, frustrated at how easily people could hide from them.

'Yes.'

'And you're telling me that no one can trace an email sent through this Tor network?' Lauren pressed for clarity. 'Surely that can't be the case or it would make solving cybercrime almost impossible.'

'Sorry, ma'am. I didn't mean to imply that. Tracing emails through a Tor network is extremely hard and not something I can do myself.'

'If you can't do it then who can?' Matt said, surprised at Ellie's admission. He thought nothing was beyond her.

'I could do it with the right equipment, but I don't have it here. You need advanced forensic capabilities to even attempt to uncover the original IP address from where the victim's emails were sent. It's tricky.'

'Do you think our forensics team will be able to uncover the address?' Matt asked, his hands clasped tightly in front of him.

'I'm not sure, Sarge, because I don't know them or their capabilities. But I do know that possibly Mac in Lenchester might be able to help us on this.'

'What, Mac?' Matt spluttered giving a hollow laugh. 'From my experience of him, he's not only overloaded with work but isn't prone to being that cooperative...' Matt's voice receded as realisation dawned on him. 'Ah... But of course. I forgot you and Mac have always had a special relationship.' He raised an eyebrow, a grin playing at the corner of his mouth.

'Yes, we do get on well,' Ellie confirmed.

'Not least because he's in awe of your talent, I expect.' Matt couldn't help but feel a glimmer of hope at the prospect of Mac's assistance, despite his initial scepticism.

'I'm not sure about that. Mac is great at what he does,' Ellie said, blushing. She fidgeted with her pen, tapping it lightly on the table. 'Shall I ask him or is that not allowed?' she added, looking at Matt and then Lauren for guidance.

Lauren turned to Matt, her expression serious. 'It's a possibility, if you think he'll agree to help.'

Matt drew in a breath, considering the options. If Mac would help, it would be great. But he didn't want to build up Lauren's hopes. 'I do know they're very busy there, so I'm not sure whether we'll get his agreement. But it's definitely worth trying.' He nodded his approval of the idea.

'Okay. In that case... yes, please, Ellie, if you could get in touch with Mac that would be excellent,' Lauren said. 'But as it's Sunday I assume we'll have to wait until tomorrow.'

'He's likely to be there. He works most days of the week, ma'am. To be honest, I think that's where he's most happy,' Ellie said, sounding in the know. 'But I'll ask him. He may well say no but if I explain the issue, he might agree to do it. And if he does, quite quickly,' she added hopefully.

A flicker of optimism ignited in Matt. If anyone could convince Mac to help it would be Ellie.

'Right, you get on with that, Ellie. And the rest of you, we've got Carmel Driscoll's husband in custody. He refused to answer any questions when we spoke at the pub, so we brought him here, and we're going to interview him shortly. Any success with the CCTV footage? Cars heading in the direction of Driscoll's home?' Lauren looked around the room, seeking updates.

Matt drummed his fingers lightly on the desk next to where he stood while waiting for a response.

'It's been impossible to find any cars going in and out of Penzance and coming from each direction because of the lack of cameras, ma'am,' Jenna said, her frustration evident.

Matt's eyebrows drew together and he let out a sigh. The lack of footage was a major setback. They would have to rely on other avenues of investigation.

'Okay, we'll keep up the search. Do we know any more about Driscoll? Anybody been able to build on what Ellie's already given us?' Lauren continued, her tone urgent.

'I'm in the process of doing a more detailed look into his social media accounts,' Jenna said, 'but there's nothing in there. He hardly ever posts.'

Matt's shoulders slumped slightly. 'What about Carmel's social media? Anything there?'

'Again, she didn't post much either, Sarge,' Jenna said.

'That's because they're both old,' Billy added.

'I don't think that's true,' Matt said. 'My parents are often on social media.'

'Aside from that, what about interviews with the victim's neighbours?' Lauren pressed on.

'I was planning to go out with Clem to do some door-knocking. But the neighbours aren't very close, so whether they saw anything or not remains to be seen,' Jenna added.

'Right. You get on with it, and we'll interview Driscoll,' Lauren concluded, setting the plan in motion.

As the team sprang into action, a mix of anticipation and apprehension coursed through Matt's veins. He straightened his jacket, his mind already racing with potential interview strategies. The interview with Driscoll could be the turning point they needed.

Except the lack of CCTV footage and concrete evidence from social media or the neighbours was an issue. They were going to have to rely on their instincts and interview skills to crack Driscoll.

Fingers crossed Ellie's attempt to convince Mac to help would bear fruit. If Mac could work his magic on the digital side, it could give them the edge they needed.

EIGHT

SUNDAY, 14 JULY

'Mr Driscoll,' Lauren began as they entered the chilly interview room. 'This interview will be recorded.'

She placed her folder on the table and sat opposite him.

Matt sat beside her and leant over, his hand bringing the recording equipment to life with a soft click. 'Interview on 14 July. Those present: Detective Inspector Pengelly, Detective Sergeant Price and...' He nodded at Driscoll.

'Rhys Vernon Driscoll.' The man sat with his arms folded across his chest, looking straight ahead but not making eye contact with Lauren or Matt.

'I'd like to confirm that you have declined to have a solicitor present,' Lauren said, staring directly at the man.

'I don't need one. They're a waste of time. And I'm not prepared to stay here until someone from legal aid arrives. It's Sunday and I'd probably have to wait until tomorrow. The sooner I'm out of this place the better,' Driscoll retorted, turning his lip up into a sneer.

'That's your prerogative,' Lauren said, giving a tiny shrug. 'Now, let's go back to yesterday. Saturday. I'd like you to explain where you were all day, right through until this morning.' She settled back in her chair, her movements measured, giving nothing away as she waited for his reply.

A look of defiance flashed across Driscoll's face. 'I didn't murder my wife, if that's what you're trying to imply. You couldn't be more wrong if you tried.'

'That's not what I asked,' Lauren said, her tone as steady as a metronome.

Driscoll exhaled loudly. 'Right. I was out all day Saturday and all evening. I left home at around one o'clock and went to The Pig and Whistle pub to watch the match.'

'What match?' Matt asked.

'Clearly you're not a local. Plymouth Argyle versus Torquay United. The annual pre-season friendly. No way was I going to miss it. And before you ask, the Gulls won. But they didn't deserve it. Bloody ref was biased as fuck.'

Matt frowned and glanced at Lauren.

'The Gulls are Torquay,' Lauren clarified. 'Can anyone vouch for you being at the pub?'

'I don't know. The place was packed, but I'm sure there'll be someone there who remembers seeing me.'

'Is this one of your regular haunts?' Lauren enquired, her thoughts racing ahead of her calm exterior.

'No. I went because they have a big screen, not like at The Bear where you can hardly see a thing.'

'Who were you with?' Matt asked.

'No one,' he answered, his voice uncertain.

Was he now beginning to take this whole situation seriously?

'So, basically, there's no one there who can vouch for you directly?' Lauren prodded, the silence of the room punctuating her words.

Driscoll gave a frustrated sigh. 'Why don't you go to the pub and ask if you don't believe me. Someone must have seen me. Anyway, they have security cameras which you can check,' he added, almost to himself, his confidence visibly waning.

'So you arrived at the pub a little while after one and what time did you leave?' Lauren asked, her tone casual, but her mind sharp, ready to catch any discrepancy.

'I don't remember going home, but I do remember watching the match and staying there afterwards drinking and...' He looked up, lost in thought.

Lauren leant forwards slightly, jumping on the change in his demeanour. 'What is it?' she asked sharply.

'Before you think this is some sort of admission, it isn't. I was kicked out of the pub.'

'For what?' Matt asked.

'Someone spilt beer on me and I had a go at them,' he confessed, his facade beginning to crack. 'The bouncer threw me out.'

'What time was this?' Lauren asked.

'I don't fucking know. Look at the CCTV,' he said, his words now holding a defensive edge. 'But I'm telling you now, I didn't murder Carmel. I was in no fit state to do anything.'

'According to your neighbour you didn't get home until the early hours of the morning. Around two.'

'Nosey bitch. She would say that,' he growled.

'Are you saying she's mistaken?' Lauren asked, tilting her head to one side.

'No. If she says that's when I got home then she's probably right.' He slumped back in the chair.

'It would help if you could remember *how* you got home?' Lauren asked, her tone even and her eyes locked onto his, searching for any flicker of deceit.

'My guess is I walked. I don't waste money on public transport or taxis. And no one would have taken me, anyway,' he said with a sigh.

'And you can't remember this walk at all?' Lauren probed further, her brows knitting together.

She struggled to believe that he could have had a total blank yet somehow managed to successfully get home.

'I'm not sure. I'll have to think a minute... I may have gone back to my car.' He rubbed his nose.

He was anxious.

Was it because they were onto him?

'So, you drove to the pub?' she clarified, not even attempting to hide her disbelief.

'Yeah. It's a long way from the pub to my house and I wanted to get a good seat.'

'Even though you knew you'd be drinking and end up over the limit?' Lauren asked, shaking her head. 'Where's your car now?' she added before he had time to answer.

'Parked near my house.'

'This is making no sense,' Lauren said, trying to make sense out of what he was saying. 'Either you walked home, or you drove. Which is it?'

'I don't know.' He tapped his fingers on his forehead. 'Okay, this is what I think happened. I went back to my car, fell asleep, and then drove home.' He nodded slowly. Actually... you know what... it's coming back to me.' He looked upwards and Lauren followed. Was his recollection genuine or conveniently crafted?

Lauren glanced quickly at Matt, seeking a silent agreement. Was Driscoll telling the truth, or simply trying to tie them in knots? It was so haphazard that she was inclined to believe he was being truthful. Hopefully, they should be able to ascertain that on the cameras at the pub.

'Okay, we'll park that for the moment. Did you send your wife threatening emails?' Lauren asked, shifting gears, and again watching his reaction closely.

'What? No.' He appeared genuinely taken aback by the accusation.

'Do you own a computer, or a laptop, or a phone? Anything with which to send emails?' she asked.

'I have a phone.'

'Do you have your phone with you?' Lauren pressed, her instincts telling her to pursue this line of questioning.

Driscoll pulled out a mobile phone from his pocket and held it out. 'Here,' he said.

'Unlock it for me,' Lauren said.

Driscoll did as requested and then passed it to her. She looked in the email sent box. There were none addressed to Carmel.

'Okay, so you didn't send her an email from this account, but you could have done using a Tor network?'

'I've no idea what you're talking about,' he said, his voice rising slightly in defence. 'Look, I hardly ever do anything on my phone apart from speak to people. And I definitely didn't send any threatening emails to Carmel. Why would I?' His jaw clenched, a silent challenge in the set of his mouth.

'Earlier you mentioned that she took everything from you, and you seemed pretty pissed off by that. I think you got drunk and anger got the better of you, so you went over to her house to threaten her and it got out of hand,' Lauren pushed, unfazed by his growing frustration.

'That's stupid. For a start, how would I've got there? Driven?' He scoffed at the suggestion.

'You say you can't remember driving home, but you did. That means there's every chance of you driving over to see your ex-wife and not remembering,' Lauren countered.

'Stop trying to pin the blame on me for something I didn't do,' he snapped, his hands forming tight fists on the table.

'You were kicked out of the force, weren't you?' Matt said, changing the subject.

'Yeah, so what?' Driscoll responded, stiffening.

'You must have resented Carmel being in the job when you weren't,' Lauren added.

Driscoll glared at her. 'Look, why I left was nothing to do with her. It was my own stupid fault. And it's also nothing to do with this.' He slammed his fist on the table, causing it to rattle.

'Calm down, or you'll be returned to the cell,' Lauren said, locking eyes with him.

'You can't do that. I've done nothing,' he muttered, the fight going out of him.

'But you know we can,' Lauren said, pointedly. 'Now back to when you were a police officer. Why were you fired?'

'I was drunk on duty and beat up one of the prisoners in custody. Which I'm sure you already know. Okay?'

'Why did you do it?' Matt asked.

'He annoyed me...' He paused, clearly reluctant to divulge the details.

'What have you been doing since leaving the police?' Lauren leant in, her attention never leaving his face.

'Mainly security jobs. I joined an agency and they send me out when they have anything. It might be to a pub, a shop, a warehouse...'

'Is this full-time?' Lauren asked.

'It's irregular,' he admitted, frustration in his tone.

'Is that because you're still drinking on the job?' Matt's question was direct, almost accusatory.

'No, it's not, Mr I-Think-I'm-Bloody-Better-Than-Every-one-Else.' The man's voice rose and his nostrils flared. 'I'm not drunk all the time.'

Was this defiance an attempt to reclaim some dignity?

'Okay, if you say so,' Matt said, holding up his hands in a conciliatory manner.

'I understand that you were violent towards your wife when you were together.' Lauren's statement came from left field and was intended to catch him out. His reaction would speak volumes.

'Who told you that,' Driscoll retorted, his face like thunder.

'It doesn't matter who. We also understand that you visited her sometimes, even since the divorce, and could get angry.'

'So what? I've got a short fuse, and she'd wind me up,' he muttered. He clenched his fists so tightly that his knuckles protruded.

'I think you visited Carmel yesterday and while you were there, she wound you up. Maybe you were drunk at the time and you let your emotions get the better of you. Am I right?' Lauren asked, her voice sharpening with every accusation.

'That's not what happened. Go to the Pig and Whistle pub. Check the cameras. Check my car. Then you'll see...' Driscoll's voice rose as he spoke and he jabbed his finger in Lauren's direction.

'As we've already mentioned, your neighbour told us that you were home by around two o'clock in the morning. That's a long time between watching a football match and sleeping in a car. You could have gone to...' Lauren's words tapered off, leaving the implication hanging heavy in the room.

'I keep telling you... check for my car. You'll see I'm telling the truth, even if I can't remember. I'm sure of it.' Driscoll's shoulders slumped in resignation and he ran his hand through his hair.

'You can stay here until we check your alibi,' Lauren said. 'Even though it's not very strong.'

'Whatever,' Driscoll said, his voice barely above a whisper.

Lauren sat back, her mind racing. His story was patchy and his alibi weak. It was both frustrating and pitiful. If Driscoll was innocent, he was doing himself no favours. But if he was guilty, then he was a man drowning in his own lies.

Either way, the truth would come out. It always did.

NINE

MONDAY, 15 JULY

'I'm sorry, sweetheart, but you were asleep when Daddy left for work and I didn't want to wake you,' Matt explained to Dani, who hadn't been up when he'd left home earlier that morning and was now telling him how upset she'd been about not seeing him.

His mum had phoned a few moments ago so he could speak to his daughter because she was very distressed after having had a nightmare.

'What time will you be home, Daddy? Can Lauren come round to see us with Ben and Tia?' Dani said, referring to Lauren's two border collies. 'I want to see them because I had a very scary dream last night.'

Dani's pleading voice tugged at his heartstrings and he wished that he could have been at home to comfort her.

'Yes, I know you did because Grandma told me. But you're okay now, aren't you?' he said, trying his best to cheer her up.

'Yes. But it wasn't very nice. It was monsters chasing me. What if they come back again?' Dani's voice quivered.

Nightmares were bad enough, but when you were only three, it would seem even worse and hard to distinguish from real life. His thoughts went back to his own childhood fears and the way shadows could twist into terrifying shapes in the darkness.

Guilt coursed through him because he wasn't there holding her close and chasing the monsters away.

'They won't come back, I promise. Grandma's there with you to make doubly sure. I'll have a chat with Lauren, and maybe we can do something soon. I'm in the middle of some important work at the moment,' he explained, his mind racing through the work in front of them and wondering if there would be a gap for them to meet with Lauren but doubting it.

'Daddy, you're always busy.'

The words stung, even though Dani didn't really mean them as an accusation. Although she was very advanced for her years, she was too young to really understand the demands of his job.

'Well, yes, that's true, but we'll see what we can arrange. We'll sort something out, soon. I promise. And Ellie from Lenchester is here, remember, and she wants to see you, too.'

'Can she see Ben and Tia, too?'

Matt chuckled to himself, wondering how Ellie would manage being out with Lauren.

'We'll see. Let me speak to Grandma and then you go and have some breakfast. You must be very hungry.'

'Yes, I am. Here's Grandma. Bye, bye, Daddy.'

'Bye, sweetheart.'

'Sorry, Matt,' his mum said after Dani had given her the phone. 'Poor thing was inconsolable, and I thought you wouldn't mind talking to her for a couple of minutes.'

'You can always contact me, anytime, day or night, you know that. It must've been a particularly scary dream. She's never had one before.' A pang of guilt settled in his chest.

Was it his job that had caused it? Had Dani overheard him talking about the case with his parents or when he'd been on the phone? He always tried hard not to let her find out anything, but...

'She was very upset and I have my suspicions regarding what brought it on,' his mum said, cutting into his thoughts.

'Which are?' he asked, intrigued, and concerned at the same time.

'When she came home from nursery on Friday, she said that one of the older children had told them scary stories that they'd heard from their babysitter.'

Matt frowned, a flicker of anger sparking inside him. What kind of person would tell stories like that to a child? He took a deep breath, trying to calm himself. 'She didn't tell me about it. And why didn't you mention it, either?'

'I thought it was something and nothing. She certainly didn't seem bothered by it at the time and didn't mention it again after she told me on Friday. When she goes to nursery later, I'll have a word with the staff, to make sure it doesn't happen again.'

Relief washed over Matt, gratitude for his mother's care and attention mixing with the ever-present guilt. 'Thanks, Mum. I really appreciate it. I don't know what we'd do without you.'

And he meant it.

'Don't be daft,' his mum said, doing her usual brushing aside any compliment he gave. 'Will you be home for dinner tonight?'

'I'll try, but with this case going on... You know how it is. I'll do my best to get back before Dani goes to bed.' He glanced up and saw Lauren entering the room. 'I've got to go; the DI has arrived. We need to get cracking. Speak to you later, Mum. Love you.'

As he ended the call, Matt felt the pressure of his dual roles as detective and father. Balancing the demands of his job with the needs of his family was a constant challenge, but moments like these reminded him of what was truly important.

'Good morning,' Lauren said, commanding the room's attention. 'I hate to say this, but we're back to square one. Driscoll's somewhat tenuous alibi holds up thanks to the manager of the pub and the fact that his car was seen on the cameras until after the murder which according to the pathologist was between nine and four.'

'But what about after he was kicked out of the pub?' Jenna asked.

'He spent the time in his car, sleeping it off. The camera shows him entering the back seat and then several hours later getting out and going into the front, after which he drove home, arriving around two in the morning, according to the neighbour.'

'No doubt still shit-faced, bloody idiot,' Billy muttered.

'There's nothing we can do about that and it really isn't important in the grand scheme of things,' Lauren said, dismissively.

'Well, that aside, how come the victim was in the barn at that time? It starts getting dark at around nine-thirty,' Billy said, frown lines appearing on his forehead.

'Maybe she heard a noise and went out to investigate,' Jenna suggested, tapping her pen on the table.

'Or maybe it was someone who had already been at her house visiting. They could've restrained her in the barn,' Matt added, trying to piece together the puzzle in his mind. There were so many unknowns.

The shrill ring of Clem's phone cut through the room. 'I'd better get this, ma'am,' he said, signalling the urgency. 'It's from an officer I know who works at Bodmin. It's strange that he'd be phoning me at this time of day when we're both at work.'

'Okay, go ahead,' Lauren said, giving her permission.

'Clem speaking.' There was a pause, and Clem's expression grew more serious by the second. 'Bloody hell. Thanks for letting me know, mate. I appreciate it.' The officer ended the call and looked directly at Lauren, shaking his head. 'There's been another body found, ma'am. By the sounds of it, the MO is the same as Carmel Driscoll. A note was found beside the body which has *Nine Green Bottles* written on it. The victim's female and she's an ex-copper who retired a few years ago from Bodmin. Her name's Jayne Freeman.'

A collective gasp went up from the team and dread coiled in the pit of Matt's stomach. One murder was bad enough, but two? And both victims with ties to the police? The case had now taken on a whole new level of urgency.

'That's all we need, someone killing off police officers,' Billy muttered, voicing the thought that was no doubt on everyone's mind.

Lauren's expression hardened. 'Thanks, Clem. Matt and I need to visit the scene. What else were you told?'

'The body was found at some allotments on the edge of Bodmin. The DI in charge of the case is Wright,' Clem responded.

'I don't recall ever meeting him, but that will soon change. While we're out I want you all to look for links between the two victims. And Ellie, if you can, please do some research into this new victim.'

'Yes, ma'am.' Ellie said.

Matt caught a flicker of uncertainty in her eyes. Was she regretting agreeing to help now she'd been thrust into the middle of *two* murder investigations?

'Come on, Matt. Grab your jacket, and let's go,' Lauren said, as he was about to have a quick word with Ellie to make sure she was okay with everything.

He'd make sure to catch up with her later.

As Matt followed Lauren out of the station, his mind was racing. Two murders, both with cryptic notes left behind. A killer targeting ex-police officers with the promise of more to come if the notes were anything to go by.

And now they were heading to Bodmin, a place he knew

held painful childhood memories for Lauren. 'You okay, ma'am?' he asked softly as they got into her car which had been parked in a space right by the station entrance.

'Yes, why?'

'It's Bodmin, and I know your thoughts on the area.' Matt kept his tone gentle, not wanting to push too hard.

Lauren's fingers tightened on the steering wheel as she started the car. 'It's not going to be easy, I admit, but we need to find out what's going on here. What we don't want is a serial killer targeting ex-police officers.'

Matt nodded, his own thoughts mirroring hers. The stakes were high, not just for the community but for the police force itself. They had to find this killer, and fast, before someone else was killed.

As they drove towards Bodmin, Matt's mind drifted back to his earlier conversation with Dani and her small, scared voice when she'd pleaded for him to come home. He sighed, louder than intended.

'What is it?' Lauren asked, quickly turning to look at him.

'Nothing... Well, it's more than nothing,' he quickly added. 'Dani had a nightmare last night and was really upset when we spoke on the phone.'

'Is she okay?' Lauren asked, sounding concerned.

'I think so, my mum has calmed her down. I hate not being there for her at times like these.'

'I get it. I might not have children, but Ben and Tia are like them, as you know. Say hello to her from me and say the dogs will be very excited to see her and it will be very soon.'

'Thanks, ma'am.'

They would find the killer and bring them to justice. And then he could spend more time with Dani and chase away the monsters, one bedtime story at a time.

TEN

MONDAY, 15 JULY

As Lauren navigated the A30 during the fifty-mile journey from Penzance to Bodmin, her eyes flitted between the road ahead and the passing countryside. The drive, though not as scenic as the back roads, still offered a comforting sense of being immersed in Cornwall's distinctive landscape and the occasional landmark, like the wind turbines, served as welcome milestones.

But despite this, she couldn't stop dwelling on where they were heading and the memories it dragged up from her younger days when Bodmin was her home. Her criminal uncle and cousins had no idea she'd returned to Cornwall. Only her aunt Julia knew because Lauren had helped her out recently when her cousins had got themselves in a dangerous situation with some of Devon and Cornwall's most notorious criminals...

'Ma'am,' Matt began, causing her to start.

Lauren quickly glanced at him, noting his worried expression. 'Yes, Matt? What is it?'

'I was wondering if you were okay. You've been clutching the steering wheel as if your life depended on it. Look at your knuckles, they've gone white.'

She looked down, surprised to see he was right. 'Oh... I was thinking about my family, and you know that always winds me up,' she said lightly, hoping to brush away his concern; they had more to think about than her paranoia regarding her relatives.

'Well, that makes sense. But don't worry. What are the odds of bumping into any of them.' He grimaced, tapping his fingers on his thigh. 'Sorry, I didn't mean to jinx it.'

Lauren turned to Matt, her brow furrowed. 'What? Jinx it? We're not at school you know.'

'Of course not... It's something that Whit—' His remaining words were left unspoken and he fiddled with the seatbelt across his chest.

'DCI Walker?' she asked, her tone a mix of curiosity and scepticism.

'Yeah.' Matt nodded, his shoulders relaxing a bit. 'She had a thing about not jinxing anything.' He offered a small apologetic smile. 'But of course I know that's not something you'd think.'

'You're right. But each to their own,' she added, not wanting him to think she was annoyed. She'd already given him enough grief in the past for comparing Cornwall to Lenchester.

'Have you given any thought to how we're going to work the case with the Bodmin lot, ma'am? Are you going to offer that we share all of our information and help each other out?'

Lauren kept her eyes on the road, her fingers less tightly wrapped around the steering wheel than before. 'No. I want both cases,' she said, leaving no room for doubt.

'Do you think that DI Wright will be okay with that?' Matt asked, not sounding convinced that he would.

'He'll have to be,' Lauren said with conviction. 'We had the first murder which means the next is ours. I'm not going to assume his reluctance. He might be very happy to hand over everything to us.'

As they drove, Lauren's mind raced with a whirlwind of thoughts. Despite the picturesque scenery they'd passed by, her attention was on what macabre scene awaited them. Her thoughts flitted back to her family. Matt was right, what were the odds of bumping into them. Bodmin wasn't exactly small, and the likelihood of crossing paths was slim. Plus, the crime scene was at the allotments and as far as she knew, neither her aunt nor her uncle, and most definitely not her cousins, were ever interested in gardening, producing their own food, or anything remotely healthy. She doubted they'd know an unprocessed food if it bit them.

The rest of the journey was undertaken in silence, the only sound being the hum of the car's engine. Once they arrived in Bodmin, Lauren parked the car close to the allotments. A mix of anticipation and apprehension settled over her and she took a deep breath, releasing her hands from the steering wheel, unclicking her seatbelt, and opening the door. Matt followed suit and together they walked over to where a uniformed officer stood on duty, alert and attentive.

Lauren inhaled deeply, the crisp air filling her lungs with the scent of freshly turned earth and the faint aroma of the sea being carried by the gentle breeze.

'No one's allowed through,' the officer said firmly, staring directly at them.

Lauren held out her ID. 'Detective Inspector Pengelly from Penzance CID, and this is Detective Sergeant Price. We'd like to speak to DI Wright. Where is he?'

'He's over there, ma'am,' the officer said, nodding in the direction of two men standing beside a battered shed with an open door.

They signed in and then headed over, taking care to walk on the pads that had been placed on the ground leading up to the crime scene. They passed several small garden plots, each one marked off by small wooden fences and in varying states of cultivation. Some were brimming with ripe vegetables and other fragrant herbs, while others were overgrown. She glanced over her shoulder at Matt. Was he bracing himself for seeing the body?

When they reached the shed, the younger and taller of the two men turned to them. 'Yes?'

'DI Wright?' Lauren asked, her tone authoritative yet open.

'That would be me,' the other man said. 'He's DS Burrows.'

Wright was in his mid-forties with a shaved head and wore a casual brown bomber jacket and light-coloured chinos. His demeanour was calm, but his eyes were sharp.

'I'm DI Pengelly from Penzance CID.'

'Ah, yes. I thought you looked familiar. I think we've met before,' he said, staring at her intently.

'Yes, that's right,' Lauren said, remembering now she'd seen him in the flesh that they'd met a couple of years ago at a ballistics workshop.

'Why are you here?' Wright asked.

'I understand you've a murder victim in the shed with a note next to her stating *Nine Green Bottles*. Yesterday, we had a similar killing, also female, only the note left beside our victim was *Ten Green Bottles*.'

'Bloody hell,' Burrows exclaimed. 'You think the plan is for ten murders?'

'I sincerely hope not,' Lauren said, squaring her shoulders to project more confidence in her opinion than she actually felt. 'What can you tell us about your victim. We understand she's ex-job.'

'Yes, that's right. She worked at Bodmin. I didn't know her. She retired before I arrived,' Wright said.

'Was the victim stabbed, and the note pinned to the floor with a knife?' Lauren asked.

'Yes, that's more or less what we have in there,' Wright said, nodding towards the open door.

'Who found the body?'

'An old boy who arrived at the allotments at nine this morning. He noticed the victim's shed door was open and thought she was in there. He went to say hello and found her.'

Lauren glanced around but couldn't see anyone. 'Where is he?'

'One of my men took him home and he'll take his statement there. He was very upset.'

Lauren would have liked to have spoken to the man but had to trust that an adequate statement would be taken. She sucked in a breath, bracing herself for resistance to what she was about to say next. 'Bearing in mind what we're dealing with, it's in everyone's best interest if I lead this case from our station in Penzance.'

'Hang on a minute,' Wright said, his arms crossing over his chest defensively. 'This isn't a decision to be taken on the fly.'

'These deaths are clearly connected, and ours occurred first, so it makes no sense for them to be investigated separately.' Lauren's hands gestured emphatically as she spoke.

'I agree, but that doesn't mean we simply hand over everything to you,' Wright said, an edge to his voice.

'I'm not saying that. We should work together on the cases, but someone needs to take the lead and it should be me. I suggest you run it by your DCI for their opinion.'

Despite the urgency to take charge, Lauren recognised the importance of following protocol and ensuring a united front, or it could hamper the investigation.

'Okay,' Wright said, with a reluctant sigh.

'Has the pathologist arrived yet?' Lauren enquired, determined not to betray any of the tension she felt inside at not knowing how the investigation was going to proceed.

'Yes, she's with the body.' DI Wright gave a sharp nod toward the shed.

'Good. I want to go inside and take a look at the crime scene. Matt, you stay outside,' she added, turning to him.

'Yes, we can't have all of us in such a small space,' Wright agreed, totally oblivious to Lauren's real reason for suggesting Matt kept away.

Lauren followed Wright into the shed, where, sitting in a corner on a chair, was the victim. The shed was dimly lit, the weak sunlight filtering through dust-coated windows creating a sombre atmosphere. Tools and gardening equipment were neatly arranged against the walls, an eerie contrast to the grim scene in front of them. At a glance, the victim appeared peaceful, sitting on a chair, but the reality of the situation lay heavy in the air.

'This is DI Pengelly from Penzance. She has a case with the exact same MO,' Wright said, introducing Lauren to the pathologist.

'Good morning. I'm Katie Jolly.'

'What can you tell us so far?' Lauren demanded.

'Nothing,' the pathologist said curtly. 'I don't believe in speculation. I'll forward my report once I've done a thorough investigation.'

'But surely you can tell us whether you believe the woman was stabbed with the same knife that's pinning down the note?' Lauren pressed, her frustration growing.

'I'm not prepared to make any guesses,' the pathologist reiterated, her tone final.

'Well, here's my card. If you could please let me know as soon as you have some details. Clearly, our two cases are linked, but it would be useful if we can discover whether or not the murders were carried out by the same person,' Lauren said, handing over her card in a gesture of formal cooperation.

'I wouldn't be able to say that without knowing the exact details of what occurred in your case.'

'I'll ask Henry, our pathologist, if he can share that with you, providing you agree to let him see your findings,' Lauren suggested.

'Is that Henry Carpenter?' Jolly asked, a spark of recognition in her voice.

'Yes. Do you know him?'

Fingers crossed that if she did it would aid their investigation.

'Very well. He was one of my tutors at university. He's one of the best we have around here, so I'd certainly be happy to discuss my case with him.'

'Thank you. I really appreciate that,' Lauren said, breathing a sigh of relief. 'If police officers are being targeted, we need to act quickly.'

'I understand,' Jolly said.

Lauren turned to DI Wright. 'Obviously, there's the possibility that the victims were targeted because they were female, as well as, or instead of, them being ex-police officers, but we don't want to speculate yet. I'd like to visit the victim's house. Has the family been informed?'

'No, we haven't contacted the family. Jayne lived with her wife, Sandra Winton, in Lanivet, which is—'

'I know the area,' Lauren interrupted, having visited the village many times when she was younger because one of her school friends lived there. 'I'm going to visit the family home now to inform the wife. You're more than welcome to come with us,' Lauren said, not wanting to delay proceedings any longer than necessary.

'Let me speak to the DCI first to get his take on how we're going to play this,' Wright said.

Assuming that Wright would want to do that without her being there, Lauren stepped outside to where Matt was standing. The cool air was a sharp contrast to the tense atmosphere of the shed.

'You wouldn't want to go in there,' she said with a dry smile, trying to lighten the mood for a brief moment. 'A lot of blood and a bit messy. It appears identical to what happened to Carmel Driscoll.'

'I'm glad I didn't have to,' Matt said, grimacing. 'Has a decision been made regarding who's leading the case?'

'DI Wright is currently speaking to his DCI. I'll be making a formal complaint if we don't end up having full control over the case, but hopefully it won't come to that and they'll see that the case is rightfully ours and—'

The door to the shed opened, and DI Wright stepped out. 'Okay, I've spoken to the DCI. He's happy for you to run the case from Penzance, but both teams will have input. We'll work together.'

Yes. She refrained from punching the air, which was hardly appropriate considering the situation.

'That's great. I'm pleased he agreed so readily.'

'We're short staffed and have two officers on sick leave. Between you and me, I think he's relieved not to have this case added to our workload. Having said that, we do still need to cooperate with each other.'

'Understood,' Lauren said. 'I suggest the three of us visit Sandra Winton and give her the news.'

'Three?' DI Wright said.

'You, me and DS Price.'

'What about me?' Burrows said.

'You can contact my team in Penzance and explain where we are with the case,' Lauren said.

Burrows glanced at Wright, who nodded.

'Okay. Leave that with me.'

'Thanks,' Lauren said, sucking in a breath as the gravity of the task ahead, of informing a family of their loss, weighed heavily on her.

ELEVEN
MONDAY, 15 JULY

Lauren followed Wright's car right as they headed towards Lanivet, the home of the second victim and as they entered the picturesque village, dotted with stone cottages, memories of her past began flooding back.

'This hasn't changed much,' she muttered more to herself than anything.

'You know where we are then, ma'am?' Matt asked.

'Yeah, I had a friend who lived around here, two streets away behind the church in the centre. I spent a lot of time at her house. It beat being at home with the rest of my family. Let's hope we don't see anybody I know.' She glanced around, a hint of nostalgia mixed with apprehension coursing through her.

'I doubt that's going to happen, as we're not exactly hanging around the streets for them to see you,' Matt said.

He was right, of course. Plus, people who lived there were hardly likely to recognise her, she'd been away for so long. She pushed the thought to the back of her mind, instead concentrating on the task at hand. Explaining to Jayne Freeman's wife what had happened.

They turned off Clann Lane into a small development of

modern houses, which hadn't been built when Lauren was last there, and came to a halt behind DI Wright outside a small semi-detached property.

'Okay, let's go,' she said with a determined nod.

They walked over to Wright's car and he rolled down the window. 'As this is now your case, why don't you break the news to Freeman's wife. It's probably better coming from you, anyway. You know... woman to woman.'

Lauren looked down at the officer and just about refrained from tutting. Talk about copping out.

'That aside, three of us explaining what has happened is overkill – no pun intended,' she said, her lips twitching in a brief, humourless smile. 'You stay here and DS Price will accompany me because he's second in command on this investigation. We'll need a family liaison officer to be with the woman. Perhaps you can arrange that while we're inside. I take it you don't have any problems undertaking that task.' She didn't bother hiding her sarcastic tone.

'No. I can do that,' Wright said, looking sheepish. He picked up his phone from the passenger seat.

Lauren headed down the short drive with measured steps, Matt close behind. She rang the bell, and after a couple of minutes, the door was opened by a woman who looked to be in her mid-sixties, with straight blonde hair reaching her shoulders.

'Yes?' she said, looking quizzically at both Lauren and Matt.

Lauren held out her ID. 'I'm Detective Inspector Pengelly from Penzance CID, and this is Detective Sergeant Price. Are you Sandra Winton?'

'Yes. Why?'

'We have a sensitive matter to discuss with you. Please may we come in?' Lauren asked gently.

'Yes, of course,' the woman acquiesced, opening the door wider to usher them inside.

They stood in the hall, a space that felt both welcoming and tense. The house had a cosy warmth, with pictures lining the walls and a faint scent of lavender in the air.

'Perhaps we should sit down?' Matt suggested.

'I'd rather you just told me what it is,' the woman insisted, her body language betraying her anxiety.

'I believe you're married to Jayne Freeman?' Lauren asked, her tone soft but direct.

'Yes,' she said, a shocked expression spreading across her face. 'What's happened to her?'

'I'm very sorry to say that she's been found at her allotment,' Lauren said.

'What do you mean, *found*?' Sandra Winton said, her fists clenched by her side. 'Did she have an accident?'

'No, I'm sorry. She's dead and we're treating her death as suspicious. I'm very sorry for your loss.' Lauren's voice was filled with genuine sympathy.

The woman stared at them blankly, a single tear rolling down her cheek. 'I don't understand. What's happened?'

'Shall we go into your lounge and sit down,' Lauren suggested, cupping the woman's elbow with her hand.

'I'll make a cup of tea,' Matt said.

'Thanks, Matt,' Lauren said.

'The kitchen's at the end of the corridor. This way to the lounge.' Sandra's voice was barely above a whisper.

Lauren accompanied her into the room and sat on the sofa, while Sandra sat opposite on an upright chair, looking dazed.

'I do have a few questions, if you're up to it?'

'Yes.' Sandra nodded her assent.

'When did you last see Jayne?'

'This morning about seven. She brought me up a cup of tea and then went to work on the allotment. It was her special place. She spent hours there.'

'Was she planning to meet someone there today?'

'No... I mean... she knows lots of people who go there, it's like a community of gardeners, so she could have, I suppose...' Sandra leant forward, wrapping her arms around her knees. 'I can't believe this has happened.'

'Was there anything bothering Jayne recently?' Lauren enquired after a few seconds, trying to tread softly.

Sandra looked up at Lauren and nodded, appearing worried. 'Jayne said it was something and nothing, but it bothered me. She was sent some emails saying that she should watch her back because they know all about her. She said it was someone being stupid and not to worry. But I think she was saying that to stop me from worrying, because she knows what I'm like.' Sandra's voice trembled and she blinked back tears.

'Had she received other threats in the past?'

'Only occasionally when she was with the police but that's usual isn't it?' Sandra looked down at her hands and fidgeted with her wedding ring.

'Yes, unfortunately, it does go with the territory,' Lauren agreed sympathetically.

Matt walked in, holding a tray which he placed on the coffee table. 'I put some sugar in yours. For the shock,' he said kindly to Sandra as he passed her a mug of tea.

'Thank you,' Sandra said, her voice soft as she cradled the mug in her hand. She took a small sip, her hands shaking slightly.

'Do you have access to these emails?' Lauren asked, once Matt had sat down on the sofa next to her.

'They're on Jayne's laptop in her study.' Sandra shook her head, her eyes distant as if she was recalling a memory.

'Where is the study?' Lauren asked, tilting her head slightly.

'It's in one of the spare bedrooms.' Sandra gestured upstairs with a slight nod.

'Please could you take us there?' Lauren asked, rising from her seat.

'Yes, okay,' Sandra agreed, setting her mug down on the tray and standing slowly.

Following her up the stairs, Lauren took in the surroundings. The house felt lived-in, with personal touches that made it feel a lot more homely than her own house. Family photos lined the walls, and a soft carpet cushioned their footsteps.

They entered a small room that overlooked the garden. A desk stood against the far wall, a closed laptop on its surface. Bookshelves lined one of the walls, filled with a mix of fiction and non-fiction.

'Is this where she did her work?' Lauren asked, scanning the room methodically searching for any clues which might help unravel the mystery of Jayne's death.

'Well, not work, really. But she liked sitting here, checking things out, especially anything relating to gardening.'

'Did Jayne spend a lot of time at her allotment?'

'Way too much,' Sandra lamented with fondness. 'She'd get up in the morning and spend most of the day pottering around. Gardening was her thing. I used to moan about it sometimes but didn't really mind.'

Lauren walked over to the desk. 'Is this laptop Jayne's or do you share it?'

'It's hers. To be honest, I'm a bit of a Luddite when it comes to technology. But Jayne wasn't like that. She was always up to date with everything.'

'Do you happen to know the password?' Lauren asked, reaching in her bag for some disposable gloves and putting them on.

'Yes, I do. It's "Welovevegetables". A little joke between us.' Sandra gave a wry smile, a brief moment of warmth in the midst of the cold reality she was facing.

'Are there any numbers or symbols with this?' Matt asked.

'Oh yes. You're right. "Welovevegetables1*".'

'Thank you. And would you mind if we take the laptop

with us?' Lauren asked, already pulling out an evidence bag from her pocket.

'No, go ahead,' Sandra consented, her voice heavy with grief yet cooperative.

'Going back to the emails that were sent, can you remember when that was?' Lauren asked.

'It was fairly recently. Over the last few weeks, I think.' The woman glanced to the side as if she was trying to recall the exact timeline.

'Were you surprised that she told you about them, considering how upset she knew you'd be?' Lauren raised an eyebrow, unsure why Jayne would mention them at all to her wife, considering her disposition.

'I came into the study and found her staring at the screen. She didn't register me being there at first and when I walked over, I saw them. So she had to tell me.' Sandra's shoulders slumped as she recounted the memory. She absentmindedly rubbed her upper arm with her opposite hand, as if trying to comfort herself.

'Did you suggest that she go to the police?' Lauren asked, as she studied Sandra's reaction.

'I did, but she said there was no need because it was someone messing around.' A pained expression crossed Sandra's face.

'How did they get her email address?' Lauren asked, her lips pursed in thought.

'I don't know. She's always had the same one, so I suppose it could have been from when she was in the police.' Sandra stared directly at Lauren as if hoping for some insight.

'Yes, that could be possible. Do you know a Carmel Driscoll?' Lauren searched the woman's face for any sign of recognition.

'No, the name doesn't ring a bell at all. Should it?' Sandra raised her hands in a helpless gesture before letting them fall back to her sides.

Lauren hesitated, not wanting to reveal too much. 'Not really,' she said, masking her disappointment with a professional nod. She didn't want to let the woman know that her wife was the second victim. At least, not yet.

'You said it was a suspicious death. What actually happened to Jayne?' Sandra asked hesitatingly.

'I'm really sorry, but I'm not at liberty to discuss anything yet because the pathologist is still investigating. But we are arranging for a family liaison officer to be with you. They'll be able to explain everything and answer any questions you have about how the investigation is going,' Lauren explained kindly.

'I understand,' Sandra said, with a sigh.

'Is there anyone we can call to be with you?' Lauren asked.

'No, not really. It's only me and Jayne. Our parents are dead. We've got friends, but I think I'd rather be on my own,' Sandra said, a mix of resolve and sorrow in her voice.

'Okay. Let's go back downstairs. Your FLO will be here soon. But if you need to know anything before then, here's my card.'

'Thanks,' Sandra said, taking it and putting it into her jeans pocket without even taking a look.

When they reached the bottom of the stairs, Lauren and Matt offered their condolences once more before leaving the house.

Walking to where Wright was standing against his car, Lauren's mind was already racing with how they were going to progress the investigation.

'Okay, Jayne also received threatening emails recently, which we need to look into. I have her laptop,' she said once they'd reached Wright.

'I'll get my researcher onto that,' the officer said, holding out his hand.

'It's okay, we can deal with it,' Lauren said, remembering they had Ellie at the station. 'How are we on the FLO?'

'She's going to be here shortly.'

'Okay, you stay here until she arrives? Our priority is finding out what links these two women, in particular if it's more than they were both police officers.' Her phone rang, and she glanced down. 'I'd better get this, it's from the pathologist in Penzance. Hello.'

'Good morning, Detective Inspector. Are you around? I'd like to go through my findings with you,' Henry said briskly.

'Yes, we can be with you in an hour.'

'Perfect. I'll see you soon.'

She ended the call, turning back to Wright. 'Right, we're off to the pathologist. I'll let you know if there's anything we can share.'

'What do you want my team to do?'

She frowned. He was being very obliging. She wasn't sure she'd be the same.

'More investigation. Speak to neighbours. Get the CCTV footage. Normal procedures. Let's see if we can find anyone who knows anything. I also want to see the statement from the person who found the body.'

'Consider it done,' Wright said.

Lauren nodded, her thoughts already on what Henry had found, hoping it would fill one of the many gaps in the case.

TWELVE

MONDAY, 15 JULY

An hour later, after a journey that had seemed much longer than it actually was, Matt and Lauren were heading down the corridors of the hospital towards the morgue to see Henry. Throughout the entire trip, Matt had been quiet, engrossed in his own thoughts. The reality of having two murders on consecutive days loomed over them, casting a shadow that was hard to ignore. Matt couldn't help but ponder the grim possibility of the 'ten green bottles' scenario. Was this the beginning of a murder spree set to last for ten days? Their leads were scarce, and the pressure was mounting. He might be well used to the burden but somehow it never got easier. Probably because his mind would run overtime thinking about all the possible eventualities.

Lauren had been quiet, too, while she was driving. He wasn't surprised because not only did she have the murders to deliberate over, but also the investigation was taking her to an area of Cornwall she didn't want to be. The tight lines around her eyes clearly showed that it was having an emotional impact on her.

'Let's hope that Henry's findings will shed some light on the case,' Lauren said abruptly, breaking the silence and startling

Matt as she pushed open the door that took them along the corridor and directly into the postmortem area.

'It has to. Why would he call us in if he didn't have something of use? Thank goodness the pathologist over at Bodmin knows him and is willing to share,' Matt acknowledged, optimistically.

He appreciated the small victories, like having a cooperative pathologist, especially considering the tightrope they were walking, between following procedure and desperately seeking leads.

Lauren nodded, her attention drifting away for a moment. 'Yes, that's true.'

'Katie Jolly was a pussycat when compared to ours in Lenchester. Dr Claire Dexter...' He exhaled loudly as his mind went back to the pathologist and her idiosyncratic ways. 'Anyone else pales in insignificance when you consider how she is... But having said that, she has a first-class reputation, both nationally and internationally.'

'Of course she does,' Lauren responded, looking directly at him.

Matt sensed she was searching for something more in his words.

'What do you mean?' he pressed, although he could guess.

'Nothing, sorry. It's just... you and Lenchester. Whenever you talk about it you say how good a person or place is. And, by implication, how lacking Cornwall is.'

Was she right? He'd been down there long enough to stop making regular comparisons, but that didn't mean he'd forgotten about his Lenchester experience. Memories didn't work like that.

'That's not my intention, I can assure you. When I mentioned Claire Dexter, who I imagine both Henry and Katie Jolly will have heard of, it's because of how difficult she could be, not because she's *better* than Henry or Jolly to work with,'

Matt explained, hoping to clarify so Lauren didn't feel so put out by his comment.

Lauren's expression softened, a sigh escaping her lips. 'Okay, I'm sorry. I didn't mean to say that. It's Bodmin – it brings up so many difficult memories. I didn't mean to take it out on you.'

Matt understood the sentiment all too well. 'I understand, ma'am. Anyway, let's hope we don't have to see anything too gruesome when we visit Henry,' he said, attempting to lighten the mood.

They arrived at the entrance to the postmortem section of the morgue and headed inside. The air was cool and sterile, very different from the warmth of the day outside. The fluorescent lights flickered slightly, casting long shadows across the room. Henry stood in the centre, wearing his lab coat and his hands on his hips. His eyes were fixed intently on the body laid out in front of him. The solemn atmosphere of the morgue, with its stainless-steel tables and the faint smell of disinfectant, under-scored the gravity of their work.

As their footsteps echoed on the tiles, he turned to face them. 'Ah, good, you're here,' Henry said, his voice carrying a mix of professionalism and weariness.

'Yes, we've returned from Bodmin where, unfortunately, there's been a similar death,' Lauren said.

'I'm aware of that. I know the pathologist doing the post-mortem on victim two – she was one of my students. She phoned a few minutes ago to discuss the case.'

'And thank goodness she was. It's only because she knows you that she's willing to share her findings without us having to wait for a formal report.'

Henry laughed. 'Yes, she was always one for dotting the i's and crossing the t's. Wanting to stick to procedure.'

Lauren glanced at Matt. 'Sounds like your Lenchester woman.'

'Don't tell me,' Henry said. 'Dr Claire Dexter.'

Matt tried to force back a snicker but was unsuccessful. 'Her reputation stands before her, I see.'

'I've attended a number of lectures she's given and witnessed her giving short shrift when asked a question that clearly indicated the questioner hadn't done their homework.'

'That sounds like Claire,' Matt said, his eyes crinkling in amusement.

'But with an expert of her calibre one should cut her some slack. It shouldn't matter if her interpersonal skills aren't the best,' Henry said.

'Okay, can we stop with the Dr Dexter accolades because we really don't have the time,' Lauren said sharply.

Matt glanced over at Henry, who was also staring at Lauren open-mouthed.

'Sorry,' Matt muttered.

'No... I'm sorry,' Lauren said, sounding contrite. 'I didn't mean to speak like that. This investigation is getting to me. What have you got for us, Henry?'

'Don't worry about it,' Henry said, with a wave of his hand. 'I want to show you the body so you can see for yourself the cause of death, rather than simply reading it in my report. My examination revealed a solitary stab wound to the chest. The knife penetrated the sternum and made a clean, precise cut through the pericardium and into the heart itself. In addition to the stab wound there was significant bruising around the entry point consistent with the hilt of the knife impacting the skin. The hunting knife, with a six-inch blade and rosewood handle, found beside the body was the one used to kill the victim,' Henry explained, gesturing to a sealed evidence bag nearby.

'How do you know?' Matt asked.

'The blade is an exact fit for the hole it created and the depth it was plunged into the body. Also, the hilt made a specific pattern of bruising around the entry point.'

'Is it an unusual knife?' Matt asked.

'I don't believe so,' Henry answered.

'Were there any fingerprints left on it?' Lauren asked.

'No. It was wiped clean. Now, if you'd like to step forward, I can show you exactly what happened.'

Matt swallowed hard, bracing himself for what he was about to be shown.

'Are you okay?' Lauren asked, shooting a glance in his direction.

Matt nodded.

He leant in slightly, observing the details Henry pointed out. The precision of the attack was chilling: a single, fatal stab wound directly to the heart. The methodical nature of the attack suggested planning – a cold calculation that was deeply unsettling. The absence of fingerprints indicated a perpetrator well-versed in avoiding detection. As he stood there, in the sombre quiet of the morgue, surrounded by the tools and tokens of death, Matt felt a renewed sense of determination. They had to catch the killer before another life was extinguished in such a brutal, calculated manner.

'Was the death instant?' Lauren asked, cutting into Matt's thoughts, her voice steady despite the macabre topic.

'Yes. There was one stab, straight to the heart, and because it was in the correct place, I would say maybe only a few minutes,' Henry replied, his tone clinical yet infused with a hint of sadness for the life so violently taken. 'However, that's not the only injury.'

'What else?' Lauren asked, arching an eyebrow.

'There's a wound to the head. I suspect that she was hit with a blunt object which rendered her unconscious. If you check the bruising on the side of her head, there's a seven-centimetre shaped mark, circling a laceration, that resembles the side of a baseball bat.' Henry gestured to the relevant areas on the body.

'Can you tell that for sure?' Matt enquired, his eyebrows knitted in thought.

'No, but there were some wood shavings in the wound which most likely came from the weapon and I've sent them away for analysis. The point is that if the victim was disabled first by the weapon, it would have made it much easier to stab her in the heart without her fighting back. Hence the clean entry wound, with no jagged edges,' Henry explained, his eyes meeting Matt's, as if wanting to confirm his under-standing.

'Was there anything to show the victim resisted the initial attack? Anything under the fingernails, or bruising on the hands or arms?' Lauren asked.

'No,' Henry said, with a shake of his head.

'Do you think that the victim knew her assailant, then?' Matt asked, the question hanging in the air, heavy with implica-tion. 'Or was she hit from behind?'

'Judging by the location of the wound it's entirely possible the victim didn't see the assault coming until it was too late,' Henry responded, his expression sober.

'So, in your view she was hit on the head, possibly hard enough to be knocked unconscious, and then stabbed?' Matt summarised.

'Yes,' Henry acknowledged.

'But we don't yet know why she was in the barn in the first place.'

'No, that's not something I can tell, obviously,' Henry said.

'Was the body moved?' Matt prodded further.

'No, I believe she was found where the attack took place,' Henry clarified, narrowing down the crime scene to a specific location.

'And do we now have an exact time of death?' Lauren asked.

'Yes, between eight and ten pm on Saturday.'

'Which means at least some of the time it would have been light,' Matt said, voicing his thoughts out loud.

'Did Katie Jolly mention anything regarding the sequence of events in Bodmin? We believe this second murder also took place outside. Unless the body was moved,' Matt continued, trying to connect the dots between the two cases.

'No. We didn't go into great detail when we spoke earlier, but I'll give her a call later for an update,' Henry said.

'Is there anything else you can tell us?' Matt asked, hoping for any additional details that might aid their investigation.

'There's nothing more to say until the toxicology report comes back, and I'm not sure when that will be.'

'If it only took one stab to kill the victim, would you say that the assailant was experienced?' Matt asked, wondering how the killer could have been so proficient.

'Not necessarily. The heart is a large enough organ for even an inexperienced person to be successful with one stab, especially if the person is unconscious,' Henry said, providing a cold, clinical assessment of the murder method.

That made sense.

'We do need confirmation that we're dealing with the same killer so if you could please be mindful of that when speaking to Dr Jolly I'd be extremely grateful,' Lauren said.

'Yes, of course.'

'Before we go, was there anything on the clothing that was out of the ordinary?' Lauren asked.

'There were some hairs that I've sent for analysis. I've been informed that she has a cat but under the microscope they didn't appear like cat hairs. I'd have thought possibly a dog.'

'How can you tell?' Matt asked. He'd always assumed the hair was similar.

'Cat hair is usually shorter, and softer than dogs'. The colouring is different, too. Individual dog hairs are a single colour whereas a cat can have bands of colour on a single strand.

I'm leaning to the hair coming from a long-haired dog. I'll confirm when I hear.'

'She could have visited someone with an animal,' Matt said.

'Or pet hairs from the person who killed her might have transferred from their clothes to hers?' Lauren suggested.

'That's a possibility, and one that might help you locate the killer,' Henry acknowledged, although there was a doubting expression on his face.

'Well thanks, Henry,' Lauren responded. 'We appreciate the early feedback. Now we need to get back to the station and find out if there are any links between the two women, apart from them being police officers.'

As they prepared to leave the morgue, a mix of frustration and determination coursed through Matt. The killer had left behind few clues, but the animal hair sparked a glimmer of hope. Could it really lead them to the killer? The thought lingered as they stepped out into the daylight, the challenge of the case pressing heavily on his shoulders.

Lauren entered the room and Matt followed as she marched up to the whiteboard and faced the team, whose focus instantly shifted towards them.

'Okay, everyone. What we've seen has confirmed that these cases are linked,' Lauren said as she wrote the name of the second victim, Jayne Freeman, on the board and drew an arrow connecting it to the first victim. 'The second victim had a note next to her on which was written *Nine Green Bottles*. Do we have anything further regarding their connection, aside from them both being ex-police officers?'

Matt glanced anxiously at the team, hoping their research had revealed something that would assist in the investigation.

'I've found something,' Ellie called out, sounding more confident than earlier. Was she now feeling more at home? Matt hoped so because if there was ever a time they needed her working at full speed, it was now.

'Go ahead, Ellie,' Lauren said, motioning for the officer to continue.

'Thanks, ma'am. Both women worked together at the Camborne station in the 1990s. After that, Jayne Freeman moved to Bodmin, where she stayed until retiring. Both were DCs for their entire policing careers.'

'Excellent. So, we can assume that they knew each other and worked on the same team. I doubt there'd be more than one CID unit in such a small place.' Lauren nodded approvingly. 'Can you tell me anything else?'

'Not yet, ma'am. But I'll continue digging.' Ellie's determination was mirrored in her straight and resolute posture.

'We need to find out the cases they worked,' Lauren said. 'It's a long shot but could be relevant, especially when considering the emails that they were sent. Which reminds me: Jayne Freeman was also sent emails. We have her laptop and password, if someone would like to check it out. Ellie, can you do that, because you can check if they used the Tor network again.'

'Yes, ma'am.'

'I'll take a look at the cases the victims worked on, ma'am, but I'm not sure how possible that's going to be. As you know, once cases are over, documentation isn't kept that long, whatever the outcome,' Clem said, his tone laced with frustration at the bureaucratic hurdles they often faced.

'Yes, that could well be an issue,' Lauren said with a resigned sigh. 'Anyway, I have more to tell you. It would appear that both victims were killed by a hunting knife with a six-inch blade and rosewood handle, which is fairly common. There are no fingerprints on the one from Driscoll, and we can assume it's the same for the other one. We need to find out if the knives were bought locally, and from where. I'll forward to you all a photo of the knife.'

'I'll get onto that, ma'am,' Billy said.

'Thanks. Turning to CCTV— Actually, before we touch on that: I want to let you know that I'll be leading the investigation into both murders but we'll be working with DI Wright and his team from Bodmin. Now, CCTV. DI Wright's team are checking footage in their area. But again, where the victim was killed, there were no cameras, so I doubt they'll be any more successful than we were.' Lauren sighed, her shoulders slumping.

'Maybe there'll be some home cameras in use that we can take a look at,' Matt suggested. 'At least there are houses close to the allotments, unlike at Carmel Driscoll's place.'

When he'd arrived in Cornwall, it had surprised him how few people had their own private security cameras. In Lenchester, police could count on footage obtained from cameras belonging to the public if there weren't city cameras in certain areas.

'Yes, good point. I'll check with DI Wright,' Lauren said. 'I want the victims' social media posts checked. Let's see if they were in contact with one another. Oh... another thing... Ellie, did you hear anything back from your forensics guy?'

'Not yet, ma'am. But I—' Ellie was abruptly cut off as Lauren's phone rang.

Lauren glanced down at the screen, a flicker of irritation crossing her features. 'Wait a minute,' she said, answering the call. 'Pengelly? Yes, sir. I'll be along in a minute.' She ended the call with a sigh. 'Okay, that was the DCI. He wants updating. So, let's get cracking on seeing what we can find.'

The room buzzed with renewed energy, each officer aware of the gravity of their task and eager to contribute to cracking the case.

* * *

Lauren left the interview room, her steps measured and purposeful as she navigated the corridor towards DCI Mistry's office. She paused briefly outside the door, collecting her thoughts and bracing herself for the conversation ahead. He would inevitably want concise reporting with no fluff. Which was fine because that was how she worked. But even so, she always liked to double-check in her head that she was well prepared.

She smoothed down her shirt and knocked on the door, waiting until he called out before entering his office.

'You wanted an update on the cases, sir.' She stole a glance around the room. It never ceased to amaze her how unlived in it appeared. Nothing was out of place. Was he like that at home? She inwardly laughed. Even if she did want to be as house proud as Mistry appeared, it would be an impossibility with her two dogs.

'I do indeed.' Mistry gestured to the chair in front of his desk and she sat down, keeping upright, wanting to portray that she was in control, even though her mind was racing with the complexities of the investigation.

'Well, it's apparent that both deaths are linked. It's been arranged with Bodmin CID that we'll run the case from here and they'll assist with—'

'Who made that decision?' Mistry said, interrupting and tapping his pen on the desk.

'I informed DI Wright that as the first death was in our jurisdiction, we should lead the investigation with their assistance. He contacted his DCI, who agreed. From what I understand they're happy to relinquish control because of their staff shortages.'

'I'm certainly aware of their HR issues. But to be crystal clear, there should be genuine cooperation between the two teams, I don't want it to be a case of us and them,' Mistry insisted, the tone in his voice leaving no doubt that he meant it.

'I understand, sir. We're part of the same overall force anyway, so there will be no stepping on each other's toes. I'll make sure of it.'

'Good. I'm relying on you to ensure we don't end up with a rift between the two stations.'

'You have my word,' she acknowledged.

'Now, please continue with your feedback.' Mistry gave a sharp nod.

Was he annoyed because she hadn't consulted him first? He was difficult to read. Anyway, she wasn't going to worry about it now. There was nothing she could do about it and she had other, more pressing, things to deal with.

'Yes, sir. We know both women were ex-police officers and they'd worked together at Camborne in the 1990s. Currently that's all we have linking the two victims.' A resigned sigh escaped her lips.

'Do you believe these murders could relate to something that occurred in the nineties?' Mistry frowned, clearly not convinced.

'I know it's a long shot but it's the only lead we have so far, and we're certainly not going to dismiss it,' Lauren explained, her hands folded neatly in front of her to mask her apprehension.

'Okay, but it seems unlikely considering the timeframe. Nevertheless, it certainly does warrant further enquiry. I understand you're an officer down through sickness,' Mistry said, his expression turning sympathetic. 'And that you've enlisted the help of a civilian,' he added.

How the hell did he know that?

Unless Human Resources had mentioned it, after Lauren had emailed them to explain that she was using Ellie and why. She'd almost decided not to let them know, because she had control over her own budget, but thought better of it, in case it was used against them in a court prosecution. She wasn't sure exactly how it could be, but barristers were a crafty lot and Lauren wasn't prepared to risk it by not doing Ellie's appointment by the book.

'Yes, sir. DC Tamsin Kellow's going to be off sick for several weeks with a broken leg. Normally, we'd be able to cope, but with a double murder to deal with it's not going to be easy. As you're aware, I've enlisted some help, and although she's being classed as a civilian in this instance, Ellie Naylor is actually a DC from Lenchester CID. She'd been visiting DS Price and she offered her research skills,' Lauren answered, wariness creeping into her voice in case he didn't approve. 'I take it HR contacted you.'

'Not specifically about this, but it came up in conversation,' Mistry said. 'I assume you're convinced DC Naylor will be useful?' Mistry's frown deepened.

He was clearly as doubtful as Lauren had been. She didn't blame him; he was only acting in the exact same way she initially had.

'Most definitely,' Lauren said with an affirmative wave of her hand. 'Previously, Sergeant Price had said how excellent she was, but I didn't believe him until I saw for myself. I simply thought he'd exaggerated her expertise because they were friends. He'd said that Ellie Naylor was the best researcher he'd ever come across – and was right. She's already proved herself. In fact, she's agreed to assist for the two weeks that she's visiting Cornwall, thank goodness,' Lauren added with enthusiasm.

'If you're convinced then I certainly won't object to having an extra pair of hands on board. Moving on, I'm planning to contact my counterpart at Bodmin, in order for us to give a joint press conference.'

'Yes, sir. Do you need me to attend?' She sincerely hoped not because her time was better used elsewhere and invariably, he fielded the questions himself and she wasn't called on to speak.

'No, we can manage that together, thank you. Make sure to copy me in on anything that might be useful.'

'Yes, sir. Is that everything?' she asked, leaning forward on her chair and about to stand.

'One more thing.'

She sat back. 'Yes?'

He rested his pen on the table and stared directly at her. 'As a rule, I don't like to interfere in day-to-day operations because I trust in your ability.'

But, she muttered inside her head. It was obvious there was one coming.

'But... staffing is my remit, and even though DC Naylor stepped in to help at the last minute, in future I'd rather you discuss appointments with me before going ahead.'

He was right. She wasn't prepared to debate the issue now, but at the time she needed Ellie to begin working straight away and didn't wish to be bothered with further bureaucracy. It wasn't like she hadn't informed HR, anyway.

'Of course, sir,' she said with a nod. 'It won't happen again.'

'Thank you. Now, it's important we solve these murders quickly, particularly as the victims are ex-police officers. We certainly don't want a further eight deaths, which is what the notes imply,' Mistry concluded, his tone grave.

'I understand, sir. Leave it with me,' Lauren assured him, as she stood up. She exited his office, determined more than ever to unravel the mystery before them.

FOURTEEN
TUESDAY, 16 JULY

Lauren made sure to get to work early the following morning. She was pleased to see that the rest of the team was also there by eight o'clock and she marched into the room.

'Okay, thanks everyone for being here early,' she said, calling them to attention with a clear firm voice. 'We've got two murders on our hands, and I'm concerned that there's going to be a third. Do we have anything new that we can work with?' She looked directly at Ellie, not wanting to diminish the work that the others on the team had done, but assuming that if anyone was going to have something, it would be her.

Ellie nodded before speaking up. 'Yes, ma'am. I've continued my research into the two victims, and the person who was in charge at Camborne during the time they worked there was DCI Warren Johnson—'

'What, Warren Johnson as in the chief constable?' Clem interrupted, curiosity etched across his face as he stared directly at Ellie.

'Yes, that's him,' Ellie confirmed.

'Well, that's interesting,' Clem said, stroking his chin thoughtfully. 'But what can we do about it?'

'We certainly need to interview him, but do we need permission for that, ma'am? I'm guessing we might,' Matt added, glancing around the room as if to gauge the team's reaction.

Lauren's mind churned as she considered the implications of the chief constable's potential involvement in the case. It was a chilling thought, one that sent a shiver down her spine.

She studied the faces of her team. They were all dedicated to their work, but this case was different. Involving a high-ranking officer like Johnson in the investigation would require a level of caution and finesse that they hadn't encountered before. That's assuming they were allowed to interview him.

'Okay, this is going to be tricky. Yes, Matt, you're right; so I need to speak to the DCI and ask permission for us to interview the chief constable. He's not going to grant that lightly. Not only that, there's bound to be certain protocols that will have to be observed.'

'Will the DCI want to do the interview, ma'am?' Billy asked. 'Because he doesn't know the case like you and Sarge do.'

'I've no idea, Billy. I sincerely hope not. Ellie, if you don't mind, continue researching Johnson from his time at Camborne. But remember' – she paused, looking at each team member in turn, ensuring she had their undivided attention – 'this has to be kept under the radar. It can't get out that we're interviewing the chief constable in respect of a murder case or all hell could break loose.'

Lauren's voice held a gravity that underscored the sensitivity of their investigation. The room was filled with a palpable tension.

'Yes, ma'am.' Billy said. 'But...' He paused a moment. 'What if he's actually involved in the murders somehow?'

'Don't even go there, Billy,' Clem said, with a shake of his head. 'The last time an officer from this force was charged with a serious crime, the bosses went crazy with tightening up procedures. We couldn't even fart without having to log it in triplicate.'

'Yikes... That would've kept you busy, Billy,' Jenna said, a smirk plastered across her face.

Laughter erupted from the other team members, and a sense of lightness floated over them for a few seconds before the sombre atmosphere returned.

'Anything further before I go to the DCI?' Lauren asked, her mind already having fast-forwarded to how she was going to explain the situation to her boss.

'One of the DCs from Bodmin got in touch, and they don't have any CCTV footage or anything from home cameras,' Clem said.

'This is so frustrating,' Lauren muttered, with a sigh. 'No CCTV. No DNA... It's like we're working in a vacuum. I take it there's nothing else.'

The officers exchanged glances, but none of them had anything further to say. The air was thick with unspoken concerns about what lay ahead and the serious implications of the chief constable possibly being involved hung between them.

'Good luck, ma'am. It's not going to be easy,' Clem finally said.

'Thanks, I've a feeling I'm going to need it,' she said, exhaling loudly.

Lauren strode out of the room and hastily made her way to the DCI's office. She knocked firmly on the door.

'Come in,' Mistry called out.

Lauren glanced over her shoulder and then stepped into his office, quickly closing the door behind her. It was almost as if she was scared of them being overheard. Which was ridiculous. They had no concrete evidence linking the chief constable to anything untoward.

So why was her gut telling her otherwise?

'Good morning, sir. Something's come up regarding the case which I need to inform you about.'

'Of course, Lauren. Take a seat. You've saved me a phone call. Before we discuss your issue, I want to quickly bring you up to speed regarding yesterday's press conference. We gave out the number of the Bodmin station for people to call with information. We made the decision for them to field the phone calls to free up your team's time so they can concentrate on the investigation.'

'Thank you, sir. That's an excellent idea and will assist us greatly.'

'Has anyone from Bodmin CID been in touch yet?'

'Not regarding the press conference, but we do know that there's no CCTV footage available.'

'I see. Hopefully someone will come forward with some useful information that will help.' The DCI steepled his fingers, resting his elbows on the desk. 'Over to you, Lauren. What's on your mind?'

She took a deep breath. 'We've researched thoroughly and have yet to find any links between the two victims other than they both worked in CID at Camborne during the 1990s. Umm... we do know that their DCI at the time was Warren Johnson – the current chief constable,' she added as if to underscore who she was talking about. Her hands fidgeted slightly in her lap and she made a conscious effort to still them.

The DCI's jaw clenched, the significance of the situation reflected in his eyes. 'Oh, I see. He's based out of the Exeter station, as you know. How do you want to deal with this?' His tone was measured, but Lauren could sense the underlying concern.

'Well, sir, firstly, all this has to be kept under the radar for now. With this in mind, I've asked my team to investigate the Camborne station in the nineties, including looking into the chief constable.' Lauren kept her voice firm despite the delicate nature of the matter at hand.

'When you say *looking into*, what do you mean exactly?' Mistry's tone was cautious, which was hardly surprising considering the delicacy of the matter.

Lauren imagined the wheels turning in his mind, weighing the implications of her words and whether or not they could come back to haunt them.

'We need to understand what was going on at the time. In particular, the cases that were being investigated and their outcomes. Clearly this is very sensitive, and my team has been instructed to confine any discussion of findings to the office.' She leant forward slightly, in order to emphasise the importance of discretion.

'Of course, yes. I understand. You're definitely taking the correct approach.' The DCI nodded, tapping his fingers on the desk, and glancing over Lauren's shoulder, seemingly deep in thought.

Lauren waited a few seconds until Mistry was paying attention.

'Obviously we need to interview the chief constable but that's not something I can orchestrate myself. I need your permission and help in arranging it.' Lauren's insides clenched at the thought of interrogating such a high-ranking officer, but she kept her composure. She'd never been afraid of facing things head-on and she wasn't about to change now. Then again, she'd never contemplated undertaking something that could have a detrimental effect on her career if she didn't do it right.

'Do you believe he could be a suspect?' The DCI's eyebrows raised, the question hanging heavily in the air.

'Currently we have no reason to believe that. My main reason for wanting to interview him is because we have no motive for the murders. I'm hoping that the chief constable might know of something that occurred during the time the victims worked with him that could help.' Lauren's tone was reassuring, despite knowing the gravity of what she was suggesting.

The DCI was silent for a few seconds while he appeared to be pondering her request.

'Okay, Lauren. Leave this with me. I'll contact the chief constable's office to see if he's available to be interviewed today.' The DCI clasped his hands together tightly on the desk. It was clear by his posture and the slight furrow in his brow that he was troubled by what he'd agreed to do.

'Excellent, thank you, sir. Obviously, we need to interview him as soon as possible, if you could please emphasise that,' Lauren said, with urgency.

Lauren was already considering the questions she needed to ask and the approach to take. She absent-mindedly tapped her fingers on her leg, the rhythm matching the pace of her thoughts.

'Yes, I do appreciate that, Lauren. But this is the chief constable we're talking about. It's not like I can demand he drops everything for you to question him. But having said that, I don't imagine there'll be any problem, he's always been very approachable during our meetings and I'm convinced he has nothing to hide. I'll get onto it straight away and will then let you know the outcome.' The DCI's words were a reminder of the delicate balance they would need to strike in their investigation.

'Okay, thanks, sir,' Lauren said, her jaw set with resolve. 'Like I said, the sooner the better. Hopefully he'll have some relevant information to help us solve this case.'

FIFTEEN

TUESDAY, 16 JULY

Matt's phone buzzed, indicating that a text had arrived. He picked it up and stared at the screen, having to read it twice because it was so surprising. It was from Ellie, who was literally sitting within spitting distance from him.

I need to speak to you.

He glanced up from his desk and looked over at her. She was staring in his direction, her expression serious and insistent, signalling the importance of her message.

Okay. In private? he texted back, seeking clarity without drawing attention to their exchange.

Yes, I think so.

What on earth was it? Surely nothing to do with the case, because everyone was aware of how that was progressing. Had she decided she no longer wanted to help them? It was, after all, meant to be her holiday that they were eating into. Then again, why not say something to him after work or at lunchtime. It was all very cloak and dagger.

He quickly scanned the room to see what the others were up to. It appeared that Clem, Jenna, and Billy were all engrossed in their work at their computers. However, Billy was fairly close to Ellie, so whatever they did, Matt didn't want to alert him.

Okay, he texted back, a plan forming in his mind. *Leave the office as if you're heading for the bathroom but instead wait for me in the stairwell.*

He sent the text and watched as Ellie read it and then casually left her desk in a nonchalant manner. She headed out of the office and none of the team appeared to have even noticed her leave.

He gave it a minute and then checked whether anyone was paying him any attention. They weren't. Quietly, he got up and headed towards the door. A surge of anticipation mixed with a hint of apprehension coursed through him. He hoped that he was wrong and she didn't want to cease working with them. But... in that case, what on earth could Ellie possibly want to discuss that required such secrecy?

Matt's brain buzzed with possibilities as he stepped into the corridor and hurried to the stairs. He pushed open the door and saw Ellie in the stairwell, her back facing him, standing beside the window, staring out of it.

'What's wrong?' he asked, his tone laced with concern as he approached her.

Ellie started, as if she'd forgotten that she was meant to be meeting him. She turned to face him, and visibly sucked in a breath. 'Umm... this could be a bit awkward.'

'Tell me. Surely it can't be that bad,' Matt reassured her.

'It's... well, I discovered something and I'm not quite sure what to do about it.

I'd know what to do at Lenchester: hand it over to the DCI. But it's different here. I don't know who to tell and what might happen if I do. It's possible that it could seriously impact the case...' She faltered, appearing uncertain and worried.

'Well, first of all, tell me. And then we'll speak to the DI,'

Matt suggested, trying to offer the semblance of a plan despite not knowing what she was about to reveal.

'It's... it's about Warren Johnson. The chief constable. Early on in his career, while still at Camborne, he was accused of sexual harassment by several women.'

'Oh,' Matt said, taken aback. It hadn't crossed his mind it would be that, but in all honesty, it didn't surprise him. In the 1990s, it went on a lot. It was a disgrace. The force had tightened up considerably since then, but harassment still hadn't been totally eradicated.

'Do you know who his accusers were?' he asked, a thought niggling at the back of his mind.

'Well, yes, that's it, Matt. Sarge. Two of his accusers were the first two victims.' Ellie chewed on her bottom lip and blushed slightly, as if somehow it was her fault.

'Oh, crap,' Matt said, his voice heavy now he knew the magnitude of Ellie's discovery and where it could lead. 'Did you find out the exact nature of their complaints?'

'Yes. The accusations stated that he'd engaged in inappropriate touching and also made lewd and sexist comments in front of them, often actually relating to them. He'd spoken about them in that manner behind their backs as well.'

What a gross, poor excuse for a human being. Lauren had thought he was okay, so either he'd cleaned up his act or had managed to hide it.

'What was done about this?'

'There was an internal investigation, and because there were contradictory accounts from the complainants, he was cleared of any wrongdoing.'

'Bloody typical. There were always cover-ups in those times,' Matt remarked with bitterness. 'It didn't help that they held an internal investigation. That wouldn't happen now, especially in matters as serious as these.'

'I know. So, what are we to do with this information? It

might not be anything to do with our case...' Ellie paused, her fingers nervously fidgeting with the hem of her shirt. She glanced away for a moment, her eyebrows lowered in concentration, before meeting Matt's eyes again. 'But, then again, what if it is?' Her voice wavered slightly as she moved awkwardly from one foot to the other, unable to stand still.

Ellie's thoughts echoed Matt's own. But it wasn't anything he could decide on. This was Lauren's domain – and he, for one, was glad of it.

'We need to let the DI know. Follow me, and when we get to the office keep your head down and ignore the others. That's if they even notice us. We'll head straight for Lauren's office.'

'Lauren?' Ellie asked, tilting her head to one side.

'Outside the office that's what I call her. She's much more relaxed outside of work. Dani loves her – and especially her dogs... There's nothing in it,' he added, though not sure why he'd felt the need to.

'I didn't think there would be, Matt,' she said softly, her tone conveying that it would be way too soon for him to be thinking about another woman. And she was right.

'Come on.' With a determined nod, they set off to confront what lay ahead, their steps echoing down the corridor with a newfound purpose.

When they reached Lauren's office, Matt knocked and pushed open the door.

'Yes,' Lauren said, looking up with a frown on her face. He knew that she hated being interrupted like this, even though he often did it. Perhaps in this instance he should have waited for her to call them in.

'Sorry to burst in like this, ma'am, but we've got something, and we don't want to make this public knowledge. It's about the chief constable.'

Matt's heart rate picked up, anticipating the impact of their findings.

Ellie explained the details, and Matt watched as Lauren's eyes widened in shock. His focus shifted between Ellie and Lauren, trying to gauge the potential fallout of their revelation to his boss.

'Okay,' Lauren said, tapping her fingers on her chin. 'It could be a coincidence that both victims had something against the chief constable. This happened a long time ago so why would it be relevant now?'

'Maybe they got together and decided to bring it up again. It's happening all the time, ma'am. Perhaps they had more evidence. Forensic testing has improved and so now things can be tested that in the past couldn't. Complaints were regularly brushed under the carpet in those days,' Matt said as he remembered the countless stories he'd heard over the years, mainly from women. They'd spoken about the frustration and helplessness they'd felt because their complaints had either been ignored, or paid lip service to. It appeared on the surface that's what had happened with the chief constable.

'That's true,' Lauren said. 'What do we know about this investigation into him?'

'From my research it appears that the investigating officers didn't do a good job. They certainly didn't go into depth regarding the complaints. Their report stated that there were contradictory witness accounts, and this led to the matter being taken no further,' Ellie clarified.

'Hmm. What exactly did they mean by contradictory?' Lauren asked.

'I believe it related to the dates and times these incidents occurred,' Ellie replied.

'Do we know how many women accused him of this type of behaviour?'

'From what I've discovered so far, at least four,' Ellie said.

Matt grimaced. The thought that there might be more victims out there, silenced by fear or bureaucracy, was chilling.

'Have you looked into the other two complainants so we can question them?' Lauren asked.

'Not yet, ma'am,' Ellie said.

'We wanted to run this by you first, before proceeding further,' Matt added.

'Do you want me to continue with this, ma'am?' Ellie asked, shifting her gaze from Lauren to Matt.

'Yes, but I want all this kept between the three of us. Depending on the interview, we may bring the subject up. But I don't think it's right to share this at the moment.'

'Yes, ma'am.' Matt nodded, understanding the need for discretion in such a delicate matter. Even if he was disgusted by the chief constable's behaviour.

'While you're here, do we have anything yet on Carmel Driscoll's laptop?' Lauren asked.

'Yes, funnily enough, ma'am, something did come in from Mac this morning,' Ellie said. 'He thinks that the emails came through a Tor network from somewhere in Spain. He couldn't get any closer to identifying where exactly but he's going to look further to see if he can get us an address.'

'Okay, thanks, Ellie. This is excellent work. Matt, we'll be leaving to interview the chief constable shortly. I've received an email from the DCI saying that he's agreed to speak to us later this morning.'

'That's great,' Matt said.

'Be ready in five,' Lauren said, inclining her head towards the door, indicating they should leave.

As Ellie and Matt left the DI's office, they exchanged a glance.

'While I'm out continue researching and find out what you can about the other women involved in the investigation into the chief constable,' Matt said, his voice barely above a whisper, ensuring their conversation remained private. He glanced around to make sure no one was paying them any undue attention. They weren't.

'Will do,' Ellie said.

'Make sure you don't leave anything up on your screen if you leave the office and keep a constant lookout for anyone trying to see what you're doing. In particular, keep an eye on Billy, because he's bound to check what you're doing, given half a chance.' Matt's concern wasn't only professional, he was being protective – of the investigation and of Ellie.

'Understood.' Ellie nodded subtly. Her voice was equally low, a mirror of Matt's cautious tone. She clearly understood the stakes and the need for discretion. 'Good luck with the interview,' she added with encouragement but also a hint of apprehension.

'Thanks. I think we're going to need it,' Matt responded, a half-smile fleeting across his face. The attempt at humour didn't quite mask the underlying tension. 'This case has suddenly taken a rather sinister turn. But we're used to that after all our years at Lenchester, that's for sure.'

'You can say that again,' Ellie said. 'So much for my well-deserved break.'

'Are you regretting it?' Matt asked, with a frown.

'No, I was joking. With you working there are only so many sights I can visit on my own, and I'm enjoying being with the team... Of course it helps that I'm being paid. So, don't worry about me. I'm fine.'

As they parted ways, Matt returned to his desk to collect his jacket and get ready to leave. He sensed that the interview with the chief constable would be pivotal and a decisive moment in the investigation. The thought was both exhilarating and daunting.

SIXTEEN

TUESDAY, 16 JULY

'How do you wish to play this, ma'am?' Matt asked as they were driving along the A30 towards Exeter where the Devon & Cornwall police headquarters was based. It was a long journey and would take them almost two and a half hours.

Lauren took a quick look in his direction and pulled a face. 'It's a tricky one. I don't know what the chief constable's like, other than according to DCI Mistry he's approachable – whatever that might mean. I've never met him in person, only seen him on telly being interviewed. I don't suppose you're familiar with him, are you?'

'No,' Matt said. 'I'd never even heard of him until now. But, in my experience of dealing with the top brass, it's not going to be easy. Especially if we question him about the harassment investigation, which I suspect he put behind him years ago with the intention of it remaining buried.'

'That's not the plan. What we want from him is information regarding the time he worked at Camborne and anything he has to say about the two victims,' Lauren told him.

'So you're not even going to mention the internal investigation in passing?'

Lauren shook her head. 'Not unless he mentions it first because it won't get us anywhere. Rightly, or wrongly, the charges were dismissed.'

She sensed Matt's disapproval but wasn't prepared to risk the chief constable turning uncooperative.

'You know it could have been a cover-up,' Matt continued. 'How often has that happened in the past?'

Matt was only voicing Lauren's thoughts, but it was too risky an approach to take.

'I agree, but if we mention it, he'll clam up and say nothing. And then get in touch with the DCI, who'll pull us off the case. It's got to be my way, okay.'

She knew that Matt wouldn't deliberately disobey her but she wanted to belt and braces it. If he did step out of line, there'd be hell to pay.

'Okay, I get it,' Matt said, with a grimace. 'But it's so frustrating that men like him can get away with that sort of behaviour.'

'We don't know that he has, Matt. We have to be objective.' Although secretly Lauren agreed with him, she wasn't prepared to admit it. 'We need to tread very carefully during the interview. Obviously, if these allegations do turn out to be the reason behind the victims' deaths, for whatever reason, then we think again. But for now we treat this as a fact-finding mission, and we need to keep the chief constable on side.'

'Yes, ma'am,' Matt said with a sigh.

They lapsed into silence after that and Lauren kept focused on the road ahead. She didn't mind the drive: it gave her time to process her thoughts.

* * *

When they arrived at the Devon & Cornwall police headquarters, they marched up to the reception desk. 'DI

Pengelly and DS Price to see the chief constable,' Lauren said, holding out her warrant card for the officer to see.

'One moment, please.' The desk sergeant picked up the phone and announced their arrival. He turned to them. 'If you wait over there, someone will collect you shortly.' He pointed towards a noticeboard several metres from the desk.

They headed over and stood, not bothering to sit on the chairs that lined the wall. Lauren crossed her arms and leant against the edge of the noticeboard, while surveying the reception area, noting its sterile efficiency and the buzz of subdued conversations. Being much larger than Penzance, it appeared more formal.

After a few minutes, they were approached by a woman who looked to be in her early fifties, wearing a dark grey trouser suit. 'DI Pengelly?' she asked, looking directly at Lauren.

'Yes.'

'I'm Val, the chief constable's executive assistant. If you'd like to follow me, I'll take you to his office.'

'Thank you,' Lauren said, offering a polite nod.

They followed her down the corridor, their steps echoing softly, and took the lift to the top floor of the building. Once out, they walked to the end of the corridor and into an office suite.

'That's where I sit,' Val said, pointing to a desk beside a large window offering a panoramic view of the city. 'The chief constable is through here.'

She led them to a closed door, gave a sharp knock and waited.

'Come in,' a voice boomed.

Val opened the door. 'I have DI Pengelly and DS Price to see you.'

'Send them in,' he said.

Val moved out of the way, allowing Matt and Lauren to enter, then closed the door behind them. The chief constable's office was large and well decorated. A mahogany desk took pride of place in the centre of the room, and filled bookshelves lined the walls. Several framed commendations and awards hung on the walls.

'Good morning,' the chief constable bellowed, rather too loudly for Lauren's liking. 'Please, sit.' He pointed to the large round table surrounded by comfortable black leather chairs in the corner.

'Good morning, sir,' Lauren and Matt said in unison.

The chief constable, a small man, maybe only about five feet eight inches tall, with very short-cut grey hair, walked out from behind his desk. He seemed to be in his sixties and was wearing his police uniform, the badges gleaming under the office lights. The deep lines on his face and the determined set of his jaw gave Lauren pause for thought. It was imperative that they tread carefully.

'This needs to be kept brief. I have a presentation to attend shortly,' he said, glancing at the gold watch on his wrist.

'Yes, of course, sir, I understand,' Lauren said, sitting down and placing a file on the table. She made sure to sit upright but relaxed, and not let him think she was in any way intimidated. 'I don't know how much you were told, but we're here to ask you about your time at Camborne in the 1990s,' Lauren began, maintaining a neutral tone but at the same time observing the chief constable's reactions closely.

'Yes, I know. Some ex-officers have been murdered.' His response was concise and gave nothing away.

'Yes, sir. We have two victims so far, Carmel Driscoll and Jayne Freeman...' Lauren hesitated for a moment.

'You say *so far*. Are you expecting more?'

'It's quite possible, sir. Our only link between them, apart from them both being ex-police officers, is that they worked at Camborne at the time you were there as a DCI.'

'I see. To be honest, their names don't ring a bell.' He seemed thoughtful, his expression neutral, yet Lauren detected a flicker of concern. 'What dates are we talking about?' he enquired.

'In the late nineties, sir,' Lauren said, staring at him, trying to gauge any hint of recognition or evasion.

'I was definitely DCI there at the time, as you correctly said. Carmel Driscoll... I really don't remember her.'

'Her name might not have been Driscoll then. I'm not sure when she got married,' Lauren added. She could have kicked herself for not finding that out from Ellie.

'So... Carmel... hmmm... I'm still not remembering,' he said, thoughtfully rubbing his chin. His demeanour suggested a genuine reflection, but it could have been a calculated pause. 'And the other woman is...?' he prompted, indicating he needed more to jog his memory.

'Jayne Freeman,' Lauren stated.

'Do you believe working at Camborne so long ago could be a factor in their deaths?'

'We're not sure, sir. But as all we can find to link them is that they both worked at Camborne, we're pursuing that line of enquiry. Can you think of a case you worked on, even after all this time, that could be rearing its head for some reason?'

The chief constable pursed his lips and appeared to be searching his memory for a few seconds. 'No, not really. It's too long ago. I have enough of a problem remembering what I had for dinner last night...' He chuckled at his own joke.

'Notes were left next to the bodies. Carmel's had *Ten Green Bottles* and Jayne's had *Nine Green Bottles*,' Lauren explained, laying out the disturbing details and bringing their conversation back to the matter in hand.

'Do you believe this is a countdown and there are going to be further murders?' the chief constable asked.

She forced herself not to groan. *You think?*

'Yes, sir. That's why we need to discover the motives. We have to stop further deaths.'

'I totally understand that, but—' He was interrupted by a knock on the door, and it opened. He frowned, clearly displeased. 'I thought I said we weren't to be disturbed,' he snapped.

A head popped around, and it was Val. 'Sorry for interrupting. Your wife is here and would like to speak to you before you head out. I did explain that you were in a meeting but she said it was important.'

'We can step outside for a moment, if you'd like,' Lauren suggested.

'Thank you. Tell Fenella to come in,' he said, returning his attention to Val.

As Lauren and Matt left the office, Mrs Johnson was waiting by the door, appearing to have overheard the conversation.

She walked past them, not even acknowledging their presence.

'Sorry to interrupt,' Lauren overheard her saying to the chief constable as she walked in the office closing the door behind her.

Lauren crossed her arms, attempting to mask her curiosity regarding what was so important that Fenella Johnson couldn't have waited.

After a couple of minutes, the door opened and the woman walked out. 'Sorry,' she said casually. 'It's all sorted, now.'

'Good,' Lauren said, being equally relaxed.

They returned to the office. 'We'll resume,' the chief constable said, not acknowledging the interruption or apologising for it.

His prerogative.

'Yes, sir,' Lauren said as they sat at the table. 'Please could you think back to your cases. I know you said you can't remember any that might come back to bite you but could you think again. Maybe there was someone you put in prison, who has now been released?' Lauren asked, leaning forward slightly to emphasise the seriousness of their inquiry.

'I can't think of anyone but I'll give it more thought and get back to you. Obviously, we need to prevent further deaths... A dreadful thing to have happened, especially to two ex-officers.'

'Thank you, sir.'

'Have you thought it might be nothing to do with their time at Camborne?' the chief constable asked.

'Yes, sir. But as I mentioned earlier, we have nothing else to link the victims,' Lauren said. They were getting nowhere. Was he deliberately leading them around in circles and not giving away anything?

'I'm sorry I couldn't be of more help. I really need to end this meeting.' He pushed back his chair and stood.

'Of course. Thank you, sir,' Lauren said, doing the same.

Their lack of concrete leads was frustrating, but she knew that every piece of information, no matter how small or seemingly irrelevant, could be the key to unravelling the mystery. She made a mental note to follow up on the chief constable's promise to think further about the case.

They left his room and returned to her car. Once they were inside and had driven away, Lauren felt it was safe to talk. She turned to Matt.

'Any thoughts?' she asked, her tone inviting an open discussion as she navigated the streets away from the station and towards the A30.

'I don't know if you thought the same, ma'am, but I'm not sure he was telling us everything. I find it hard to believe that he can't remember anything from his time at Camborne. He was being evasive. Whether it's knowing about the charges against him that's affected my judgement, I don't know. But he seemed... trying to cooperate but without telling us anything. Because let's face it, he told us nothing.'

'He also didn't seem overly upset by the murder of the women, who were once officers in his charge,' Lauren added.

'I agree. But...' Matt said, pausing as if wanting to choose his words carefully. 'Despite all this, it's not cause for us to assume that he was involved in the deaths.'

'His wife seemed nice. Not what I'd have expected,' Lauren added.

'In what way, ma'am?'

'Oh, I don't know. She seemed like a normal friendly person and not at all up herself like he clearly is,' Lauren said.

'Yes, interesting that he made time to talk to her, even though it was in the middle of the meeting. Perhaps she wears the trousers in the relationship, despite how she seemed,' Matt suggested.

'Well, he didn't have much choice, as he was going out afterwards,' Lauren pointed out. 'Although he could have asked her to wait, I suppose. Anyway, there's little point in discussing his wife because we're hardly likely to come across her again. Let's get back to the station and report back to the team.'

SEVENTEEN

WEDNESDAY, 17 JULY

Matt had left home early, but not before ensuring that Dani was okay and she hadn't had another nightmare. He arrived at the office before anyone else, but before he'd had time to sit down at his desk, the phone's insistent ring cut through the quiet. 'DS Price,' he answered briskly.

'Matt, it's Roy,' the desk sergeant said, a sense of urgency threading through the words. 'We've got another body. A male, Craig Garland, was found at his home by his cleaner. A call came in earlier this morning, before I came on duty, and two officers were sent out to Madron. They've just reported in. From what they told me, it's looking like the same MO as the previous two bodies.'

A cold, sickening fear crept through Matt's veins. The nightmare scenario they'd desperately hoped to prevent had happened and they'd been helpless to stop it.

'Thanks, Roy.' The gears in his mind turned as he pieced together the scant information. How many more lives would be lost before they could stop this monster?

Without even bothering to hang up his jacket, he headed straight to Lauren's office. He could see that she was there from the shadow through the glass. He tapped on the door and without waiting for a response, pushed it open.

'Yes?' Lauren said, her eyebrows raised in mild surprise at his abrupt entrance.

'We've got another body, ma'am. Craig Garland. This time in our area. Madron. He was found by his cleaner. Same MO, I believe.'

Lauren tensed. 'We expected it might go this way. But it doesn't make it any easier. Have you told anybody else?'

'Not yet, ma'am. I'm the only one here.' Matt glanced at his watch. 'It's early for the cleaner to have arrived, discovered the body, and then phoned it in. She'd have had to have been there at least forty minutes ago, I'd have thought. That makes it seven. Do cleaners start that early?'

He'd never had a cleaner. When he'd suggested it to Leigh one time, prior to Dani being born, because they were both working full time, she'd dismissed the idea, saying she'd rather do it herself. She said she found it therapeutic.

'We'll find out more when we get there,' Lauren said, bringing him back to the present. 'Let's go.'

He glanced back at the office and noticed Ellie heading to her desk.

'I'll ask Ellie to look into him, before we go.'

He returned to the office and headed to the officer's desk.

'Hi, Matt,' Ellie said, as she hung her bag on the back of the chair and pulled the keyboard towards her.

'Morning. We've got a third body, I'm afraid. Craig Garland, who lives in Madron. See what you can find out about him. When the others arrive, please ask them to start digging, too.'

'What exactly shall I say to them?' Ellie asked, a panicked expression crossing her face.

He'd forgotten how nervous she could get when dealing with people she didn't know well.

'Explain what's happened, and that the DI and I have gone to the scene. They'll know themselves what they have to do,' he said, wanting to reassure her.

He hoped his calm demeanour would help put Ellie at ease. Despite being so capable, she often needed a boost of confidence. He'd check in with her later to make sure she was handling everything okay.

Madron was a little under two miles from the station, which meant a short journey. Sitting in the passenger seat, Matt stared out of the window, watching the morning light paint the sky in soft hues of pink and orange. The streets were still relatively quiet.

The landscape became more rural once they'd left the town centre. Lush green fields stretched out on either side of the road, dotted with the occasional farmhouse or grazing sheep. The winding country lanes were lined with ancient stone walls, their surfaces covered in a patchwork of moss and lichen.

As they neared their destination, the familiar tension that came with approaching a crime scene settled over Matt. The tranquil beauty of the Cornish countryside was at odds with the task that awaited them. With a deep breath, Matt concentrated on the job in hand as Lauren drew the car to a stop outside the semi-detached, white rendered house where the crime took place.

The area was cordoned off and PC Sam Riddell stood at the door, the gatekeeper to the grim scene inside.

'Morning, ma'am. Sarge,' Riddell greeted as they approached.

'Constable,' Lauren responded, formally. 'Where's the body?'

'In the kitchen. There's a note, pinned to the wooden floor with a knife.'

'So, exactly the same as the other two,' Matt observed, turning to Lauren.

'Yes,' Lauren said with a sigh. She returned her attention to the constable. 'I understand the cleaner found the body. Where is she and do you know why she was here so early?'

'Mrs Kempthorne the cleaner is at the neighbour's house with Amy – PC Smith,' Riddell said, gesturing to the adjoining house. 'Mrs Kempthorne got here early to let out the dog. She thought the victim wouldn't be there.'

'Finding him dead would have been a huge shock,' Lauren remarked.

'Yeah,' Riddell agreed. 'It clearly was. By the time we arrived she was bordering on hysterical. It took a while but we managed to calm her down. Well, Amy did most of the calming. She's much better at that sort of stuff than me.'

Matt glanced at the burly officer standing beside him. At over six feet tall, with broad shoulders and a stern expression, Riddell didn't seem like the type of man to have a softer side, although Matt suspected there might be by the way he mentioned Amy's comforting skills.

'Has the pathologist arrived yet?' Lauren asked, returning to the present.

'Yes, ma'am, Dr Carpenter arrived a few minutes before you.'

'Okay, we'll go through. Unless you'd rather stay outside, Matt?' Lauren asked, turning to him.

He appreciated her consideration but he'd decided last night, when dwelling on the possibility of there being more deaths, to face every situation they came across. Whitney had always been conscious of his issue with anything gory, but now with Lauren he was determined not to let it define him.

'No, no, it's fine.' Matt sucked in a breath. 'I'll come with you.'

They walked into the hall, past the two cupboards along

one side, and down to the open-plan kitchen-dining area which ran along the full width of the house. Beside the dining table and chairs, a door led to the rear garden.

With camera in hand, Henry was crouched down beside the body on the floor, close to the sink.

'Morning, Henry.' Lauren stopped about a couple of metres from where the pathologist was working.

'Morning,' Henry responded, his tone sombre. 'Body number three.' He stood up and gestured for them to head over to where he was standing.

Matt took a deep breath and forced himself to follow Lauren, taking several hesitant steps forward until they could see the victim. A wave of nausea washed over him. The victim was laid on his back with his arms by his side, his lifeless eyes staring up at the ceiling. A pool of dark blood had formed around the centre of his chest. Beside him, a note was pinned to the wooden floor with a knife.

'We now have a serial killer,' Lauren stated, her voice cutting through the heavy silence of the room. She turned to Henry. 'What can you tell us so far?'

Henry cleared his throat. 'It appears identical to the other deaths. I've been in touch with Katie Jolly at Bodmin, and we've compared notes. Her death was identical to our first and, I suspect, this one. Same type of knife used with no prints. Same method of killing. Same note in respect of paper, font, and words – well, more or less. We have *Ten* and now *Eight* and she has *Nine*. There were no forensics found on the Bodmin note either.'

Matt's stomach plummeted at the thought of a serial killer being on the loose. He glanced around the room, trying to look at anything other than the lifeless body on the floor. On the dining table he noticed a laptop.

'There's his laptop, ma'am,' he said, pointing to the table. 'Shall we take it?'

Lauren nodded. 'Yes, there might be something on there we can use.'

'I'll bag it.' Matt walked over to the table, grateful to have something else to do other than stare at the victim. He pulled on a pair of gloves and carefully placed the laptop into an evidence bag, sealing it tightly.

'Henry, do you have a time of death yet?' Lauren asked.

'Eight pm to midnight. But I'll let you know more precisely after the postmortem,' Henry said, his tone reflecting the seriousness of the situation.

'Have any results come back from the first body?'

'Yes, late yesterday evening. Nothing untoward found in the woman's blood. So she wasn't drugged, which I didn't think anyway. The animal hair is from an English Setter.'

Lauren nodded, her expression grim. 'Thanks, Henry. We'll leave you to it and go next door to speak to the woman who found the body.'

EIGHTEEN
WEDNESDAY, 17 JULY

The door to the victim's neighbour's house was answered by PC Smith.

'We're here to speak to Mrs Kempthorne,' Lauren said to the young officer.

'She's in the lounge with the woman who lives here, ma'am. Follow me.'

'Thanks.'

As they entered, Lauren quickly scanned the area, taking in the abundance of knickknacks that filled every available surface. It was such a contrast to the house next door.

'Ma'am, this is Mrs Kempthorne, who works for the victim,' Smith said to Lauren, gesturing to the woman sitting on the grey leather easy chair, a mug in her hands.

'I'm Dee and I live here,' the other woman said, as she jumped up from her seat on the sofa.

Lauren offered a polite smile. 'We'd like to speak to you shortly. For now, please could you leave us,' she said, her tone firm but not unkind.

'Yes, of course,' Dee said. 'I'll wait in the kitchen.'

Lauren turned to the officer who was standing beside her.

'You can go now, too, PC Smith. I'm sure PC Riddell could do with some assistance.'

'Yes, ma'am.'

Once they were alone, Matt and Lauren sat down on the sofa, facing Mrs Kempthorne. Lauren leant forward slightly, her elbows resting on her knees as she studied the woman. She appeared shaken, and her hands trembled slightly as she clutched the mug.

'How are you feeling? It must have been a shock,' Matt said, his voice gentle and empathetic.

'It was,' the woman said, sniffing, her eyes glistening with unshed tears.

'Are you up to answering a few questions?' Lauren asked, reaching out and placing a comforting hand on the woman's arm.

'Yes.' Mrs Kempthorne nodded, taking a deep breath to calm herself.

'Have you worked for Mr Garland long?' Lauren asked, wanting to piece together the victim's life and routines.

'I've been with Mr G about five years. I clean for him twice a week, and often there are other jobs he needs doing. He's not very mobile because of his arthritis.'

Lauren nodded. Five years was a long time which meant she must have known the victim well.

'How does he manage with his dog, being so immobile?' Matt asked, his head slightly tilted to one side.

'It's not bad all of the time. When his arthritis does flare up, he can't walk very well, but Rufus is old and can go out into the garden. He doesn't need long walks...' She paused, her mouth opening with sudden realisation. 'Oh no. What's going to happen to Rufus?'

Lauren exchanged a glance with Matt, a silent understanding passing between them.

'Don't worry about that, we'll sort it out,' she assured Mrs Kempthorne, her voice calm and confident.

'I didn't see the dog in the house?' Matt said, his eyebrows raised in question.

'He's in the garden. I heard him barking when I arrived. He must have been there since Mr Garland died. I didn't let him in.'

Lauren leant back against the sofa, her arms resting by her side as she considered this new information. The dog could have been a witness. Not that it could help them, unfortunately. She also remembered what Henry had said about the dog hairs on their first victim.

'What breed is Rufus?'

'He's a Yorkshire Terrier.'

Short-haired. So no link.

'I see. Thank you. Can you talk us through what happened this morning?' Lauren asked, keeping her voice gentle so as not to upset the woman further.

Mrs Kempthorne nodded, her fingers tightening around the mug in her hand. 'I arrived early at seven thinking that Mr G wouldn't be there. I called out for Rufus but he didn't come. Which was strange because he's always there to greet me. So, I went into the kitchen and saw Mr G lying there. That's when I heard barking from outside. I stood there for a couple of seconds and then left the room and phoned the police. I stayed in the hall until they arrived.' Her voice shook, clearly the memory of the discovery still fresh in her mind.

'You did very well,' Matt said. 'It can't have been easy.'

'Thank you. It wasn't,' Mrs Kempthorne said, glancing down to the floor.

'Does Mr Garland have any family we can call?' Lauren asked, her mind having already moved on to the next line of questioning.

'Not that I know of. His wife died of cancer a few years ago

and they didn't have any children. Well, that's what he told me.'
Mrs Kempthorne's expression was uncertain.

Lauren's brow pulled together, her instincts telling her
there was more to the story. 'Was he worried about anything
recently?'

'He was, yes. It was to do with his old job. He used to be in
the police, like you,' Mrs Kempthorne replied, looking directly
at Lauren.

'Do you know what was bothering him?'

'He was worried when he heard about the deaths of the two
other officers that were announced on the telly.'

'What did he say about it?' Lauren pressed.

'He told me that he could be next.'

Lauren's heart rate increased. 'Really? Did he tell you why?'

'No. I thought he was being a bit overdramatic. That's what
he's like sometimes. He did like to exaggerate. And I thought
maybe it's one of his stories. I said to him, why don't you speak
to the police about it, then? He said no because he couldn't trust
them.' The woman's fingers fidgeted with the mug, her unease
evident.

Lauren shared a look with Matt. Were they finally getting
somewhere?

'Did you ask why he felt like that?' Lauren asked, her
expression serious.

'I did, but he wouldn't really say.'

Matt raised an eyebrow. 'What do you mean by *really*?'

'He said it's something to do with what happened nearly
thirty years ago, and the police are involved.' Mrs Kempthorne's
voice was barely above a whisper, as if she was sharing a secret.

Lauren's mind reeled with the implications of this new
information. 'Were you worried by what he'd said?'

'Well, no. Because like I said, I thought it was him making it
into something it isn't. That's what he's like, see.' The woman

glanced at her watch, a hint of urgency in her movement. 'Look, I've really got to go now because I'm due at another job.'

Matt's brows raised in surprise. 'You're going to carry on working today, after all this?'

'I have to. It was awful finding him, but I need the money. My husband's been out of work for nearly a year, and there's all the bills to pay.'

Lauren nodded, understanding the woman's predicament. She reached into her pocket and pulled out a card. 'Yes, of course, you may go, but we might need to question you again. Take this. Contact me if you think of anything else that might help us,' she said, handing the card to her.

'Thank you,' Mrs Kempthorne said.

They saw the woman to the door and then headed to the kitchen, their footsteps echoing in the quiet house. Dee was sitting at the kitchen table, staring at the phone in her hand, her fingers swiping across the screen. Lauren cleared her throat softly, drawing the woman's attention. 'May we have a few words?' she asked, politely.

Dee looked up, a flicker of surprise crossing her features. 'Yes. I thought you'd be longer with the cleaner. Sit down. Would you like a drink?' she offered, while gesturing to the empty chairs.

Lauren shook her head, her hands clasped in front of her. 'We're fine, thanks.' She took a seat opposite the woman. 'How well did you know Mr Garland?'

Dee set her phone down on the table. 'Not well at all. We only moved here a few months ago. We'd say hello if we saw each other outside, but that wasn't often.'

'Do you live here alone?' Matt asked.

'No. My husband lives with me but he's away for work this week so I'm on my own.' Dee's fingers tapped on the table, her gaze drifting to the window.

'Did you hear anything last night between eight and midnight?' Lauren asked.

Dee shook her head, an apologetic expression on her face. 'No, sorry. I was in bed by nine and went straight to sleep. I've always gone to bed early. It drives my husband mad because he's the total opposite. He'll stay up until the small hours. If he'd been here then he might have seen something... Sorry about that.'

Damn. How annoying that he was away.

'Have you noticed anything strange recently? Anyone hanging around the area who shouldn't be for example?' Lauren asked.

Dee shook her head. 'Sorry, no. Although I work from home, my office faces the garden, so I don't notice anything going on out the front.'

Clearly Dee had little to offer in terms of useful information so Lauren reached into her pocket and pulled out another card, sliding it across the table towards the woman. 'That's fine. Thanks for your time. If you do think of anything that might help, please give me a call.'

Dee nodded, picking up the card and turning it over in her fingers. 'Of course, I will.'

With that, Lauren and Matt stood up, their chairs scraping against the tiled floor, and left the house, the cool morning air hitting their faces as they stepped outside.

On their way to the car, Lauren was already considering their next steps. 'We need to get back to the office,' she said, her tone business-like.

Matt nodded, falling into step beside her. 'Yes, ma'am. You know, now we have a male victim, does that mean the chief constable's harassment accusations are no longer relevant?' he asked, his brow furrowed in thought.

Lauren paused, resting her hand on the car door handle.

She turned to face Matt. 'We still need to consider them, but it does appear that they might not be the motive.' Her voice trailed off as her thoughts lingered on the scene before them, the reality of their task weighing heavily as they prepared to leave.

NINETEEN

WEDNESDAY, 17 JULY

Lauren stepped into the office, her breathing shallow as she endeavoured to calm herself down – but barely masking the storm of thoughts swirling in her head. Three bodies in a matter of days. How many more were they going to find before they could solve this crime and discover who was behind it? It was becoming increasingly likely that the murders were linked to the police force in some way, but how was anyone's guess – which didn't bode well for the investigation.

As they stood beside the whiteboard, Lauren's determination hardened.

'Listen up, everyone,' she said with a voice that cut through the low hum of conversations and the clatter of keyboards. Glancing around the room, the expression on each member of the team's face reflected a mix of concern and anticipation. 'We've just got back from the latest crime scene. Our third victim, as expected, had the note *Eight Green Bottles* beside his body. It goes without saying, but I'm going to say it anyway... if we don't solve this case soon, we're going to end up with more bodies on our hands.' She paused, letting the gravity of her words sink in. The room was pin-drop silent, every officer hanging on her next words. 'Right, what do we know so far?' She scanned the room.

'Ma'am,' a voice called out. It was Ellie, her hand raised and her tone carrying a mix of urgency and insight. 'Craig Garland was also stationed at Camborne, at the same time as the other two victims. He was a DI.'

Lauren nodded, a flicker of hope sparking within her. 'Thanks, Ellie,' she said, her voice warm with appreciation. 'I think we can definitely assume that Camborne is our link. Did you discover anything further about him?'

'Yes, ma'am, but it's complicated...'

Lauren frowned. 'In what way?'

'Could you come over here,' Ellie said, her voice barely audible.

Lauren marched over to the young officer's desk. 'What is it?'

'Garland was a corroborating witness in the chief constable's sexual harassment investigation. He confirmed Carmel Driscoll's account of one particular incident,' Ellie said quietly.

'What was that?' Billy exclaimed.

Damn. Not quiet enough.

Panic crossed Ellie's face. 'Sorry,' she muttered, looking down at her desk.

Lauren looked at each member of the team in turn, all of whom were staring in their direction, clearly having overheard Billy. 'Okay. What I'm going to tell you remains in this room and goes nowhere. There was an investigation into sexual harassment by the chief constable when he was a DCI at Camborne. The charges were dismissed. Ellie, how was Garland involved exactly?'

'He'd overheard the DCI making a comment but because he wasn't in the actual room at the time, it was disregarded.'

'Bloody ridiculous,' Jenna muttered.

Lauren couldn't have agreed more.

'So... where does that leave the chief constable in respect of our investigation?' Clem asked, his question echoing Lauren's thoughts.

'Right in the thick of it, I'd say,' Billy responded, with a wry grin.

Lauren held up a hand. 'Not necessarily,' she cautioned, not wanting them to point fingers without any evidence.

They had to be careful.

'If he's not involved, then could he be in danger?' Jenna asked.

'It's a possibility, but we need to understand the motive before making that assumption. What else has been discovered in our absence?' She scanned the room, her eyes resting on Ellie.

Ellie sat up straighter in her chair, her hands clasped in front of her on the desk. 'Quite a lot, ma'am. First of all, I looked into the song "Ten Green Bottles", which I know we associate with being a children's rhyming song. But one suggestion is that it comes from the London underworld in the old days and referred to officers from the Met.'

'Yes, that's right,' Clem muttered in agreement. 'Although calling police "bluebottles" dates back from the sixteenth century... but the song refers to them as green and this—'

Billy turned to him, his face incredulous. 'Why didn't you tell us this before?' he demanded, his voice rising in disbelief.

'I don't know,' Clem said, his voice apologetic, hanging his head. 'It wasn't until Ellie mentioned it that I suddenly remembered.'

'It's your age, mate. You know it's downhill all the way,' Billy teased.

Jenna glared at Billy. 'Oi, less of that. I'm older than Clem, remember.'

'But you don't act it,' Billy said, cheekily.

'I'm really sorry, ma'am,' Clem said, turning to Lauren.

A flash of irritation coursed through her. 'Well, make sure you don't forget again,' she snapped.

She immediately regretted her tone, and that was before catching sight of Matt's frown in her direction.

Damn. Had she undone all the progress she'd made with the team recently with one slip of the tongue?

'Sorry, ma'am,' Clem repeated.

'No need to apologise. It's me who should be sorry,' she said, her voice softening. 'We know now what it means. We need to find out if there was an investigation between the Met and the Devon & Cornwall force, in particular Camborne.'

'I'm on that already, ma'am.' Ellie spoke up, her voice laced with a hint of excitement.

Lauren's eyes widened in surprise, her earlier tension momentarily forgotten as Ellie's words sank in. What a find the young officer was. She'd make an incredible asset to any team.

'I told you she was good,' Matt said, smiling in Ellie's direction, sounding like a proud parent.

The others in the room shared glances, their expressions softening into grins directed at Ellie, who blushed deeply under the attention. A smile tugged at Lauren's lips, the recent tension in the room dissipating as they continued to focus on the progress they were making.

'During the 1990s, 1997 to be exact,' Ellie continued, returning to the matter at hand, 'the Met provided a tip-off to the Devon & Cornwall Police, in particular Camborne about a violent London gangster who was hiding out in Cornwall under a false name.'

Lauren leant forward, her curiosity piqued. 'Good gracious, how did you discover that?' Lauren asked, her voice filled with admiration.

'It took some digging into several police databases, ma'am. They're accessible, but you need to know where to look.' Ellie shrugged modestly.

'And what happened to this gangster? Where—'

'His name was Ronald Whitlock,' Ellie interrupted. 'Although in Cornwall, he was known as Raymond White. He ended up being extradited to Madrid and tried for several murders in Spain. He was found guilty and imprisoned for life.'

'That's interesting,' Lauren said, tapping her chin thoughtfully. Whatever was going on, there was now every chance of it turning into an international case. Would she even be allowed to continue as senior investigating officer? She hoped so, but you couldn't be sure. She certainly wasn't going to pose the question to her superiors. For now she'd continue with it.

'But how does that case from all those years ago link to our murders? It makes no sense to me,' Billy said, shifting in his seat, his forehead creased in confusion.

Jenna nodded in agreement. 'Same for me,' she said, her tone echoing the room's growing intrigue.

'Well, I don't know if this is linked,' Ellie added cautiously, 'but Whitlock was recently found dead in his cell.'

The room fell silent as they all absorbed this new information. The atmosphere was charged with a mixture of shock and speculation.

'When you say *recently*, how recently?' Matt asked, breaking the silence.

'About a month ago. So it was before our first murder,' Ellie clarified.

'What do we know about it?' Lauren asked urgently.

'I couldn't find much,' Ellie replied, frustration in her voice. 'I don't know whether it was from natural causes, murder or suicide.'

'It's important to know, I reckon. How do we find out?' Billy drummed his fingers on the desk, his question hanging in the air.

'You need to contact Europol,' Ellie suggested, her hand

gesturing towards Lauren. 'They'll put you in contact with someone who can give you more information about the death.'

Lauren gazed warmly at Ellie. 'Thanks. I don't think we would have got so far so quickly without your input.'

Ellie ducked her head, a modest expression on her face as she unconsciously stroked her arm, clearly pleased with the recognition. 'That's okay, ma'am.'

The breakthrough, though daunting, presented a new path to follow and Lauren was filled with a renewed sense of purpose. The pieces of the puzzle were beginning to form a clearer picture. They were one step closer to understanding what was going on. But that didn't mean they could get complacent. There was still a lot to be done. And the distinct possibility they'd be facing further deaths.

'Okay. Ellie. I'd like you to find out, if you can, the people on the team of the operation to arrest Whitlock,' Lauren said.

'Ma'am, I've already done that,' Ellie responded immediately. 'There were ten people from Camborne who worked on the case, and that included the DCI, who's now the chief constable. Out of those ten people, there are seven left when we discount the three who have been murdered. And out of those seven, two have died; three are living overseas; one, Nancy Swift, I've yet to trace; and the other is the chief constable,' Ellie recited.

Billy shook his head, his expression serious. 'So, you were right, Jenna. The chief constable could be in danger.'

'Possibly,' Matt said with caution. 'But now isn't the time to start assuming.'

'Shouldn't we warn him?' Jenna asked, urgently, looking directly at Lauren. 'He might be a sleazeball if these harassment charges are right, but he does need to know.'

Lauren considered her words. She was right, but they needed to be sure before raising the alarm.

'I'd like to have more information before doing that in case we're wrong. I'm going to contact Europol and find out what went on in this Spanish prison and the circumstances of Whitlock's death.'

'What do you want the team to do, ma'am?' Matt asked.

'Investigate further into the victims. Now we have a potential link that might help. I also want CCTV checked. Again, there are no cameras in the vicinity of Craig Garland's house. But you might notice the same car heading in the direction of each one, even if footage ceases before actually getting there. Also, contact Garland's neighbours to see if there are any house cams, and if anyone saw anything. Ellie, if you can please text me the Europol details I'll contact them now. And thanks for your input. I think I can speak for all of us when saying that your input has been invaluable.'

'More like mind-blowing,' Billy said, grinning. 'Are you sure you're not a robot? Some artificial intelligence... someone sent from outer space...'

'Billy, that's enough,' Matt warned, frowning in his direction, his voice stern and his expression disapproving.

'I'm only joking, Sarge. Ellie knows that, don't you?' Billy held up his hands in a placating manner.

He winked in Ellie's direction and she went a shade of pink. What was that all about?

'Yes. It's fine, Matt— Sarge,' Ellie said, her expression amused.

Matt's frown softened. 'That's okay, then. As you were.'

The room erupted in laughter, the tension momentarily broken.

Lauren left the room for her office, already thinking ahead to their next moves, the potential leads they could follow, and the obstacles they might face. Not to mention the involvement of the chief constable. They had a lot of work to do. Without Ellie's diligent work, there was every chance that they'd be facing a lot more deaths. She shuddered at the thought.

TWENTY
WEDNESDAY, 17 JULY

Lauren sat at her desk, grateful that Ellie had given her the contact details of someone at Europol because it would have taken her an age to find the right person to contact. She was unsure how Ellie had managed to obtain the details so quickly but wasn't going to ask. Some things are best left unchecked. A slight smile tugged at the corner of her mouth as the thought went through her head.

Who was she?

She'd never been so laissez-faire before. It had to have been Matt's fault.

Lauren hadn't had anything to do with Europol before. She knew it was an agency for the European Union for law enforcement, linking all European Union countries, and often non-member countries, to deal with crime across Europe – including terrorism, drug trafficking, human trafficking, and other cross-border crimes. But that was about it. She'd never come across anyone who worked there.

Luckily the person she'd been put through to at Europol spoke excellent English and had given her the name of someone in the Guardia Civil, the Spanish national police force. She had put a call through to Manuel Alonso and was now waiting for him to call her back. Hopefully he would also speak English because her knowledge of Spanish was limited to *hola, adiós*, and *por favor*. Hello, goodbye and please.

Lauren's fingers tapped against the desk, impatient to receive the call. Maybe she should ask Matt to join her, so he could listen to the conversation. She picked up her mobile from her desk. *Come to my office NOW*, she quickly texted him.

Within a few seconds, there was a knock at the door, and he walked in.

'Yes, ma'am?'

Lauren looked up, meeting Matt's eyes. 'I'm waiting for Manuel Alonso from the Guardia Civil, which is the Spanish police, to call me back. It's useful for you to be here, too.'

'Yes, ma'am. Good idea,' Matt said.

'You don't speak Spanish, by any chance, do you?'

'Not a word.' Matt pulled out the chair in front of Lauren's desk and sat down.

Before she had time to comment, her phone rang. She glanced at the screen. It was an international number.

'This must be him,' she said, her heartbeat quickening with anticipation. 'DI Pengelly speaking.'

'Hello, I'm Manuel Alonso,' he said in a cheery voice. 'I've been asked to give you a call regarding one of our prisoners.'

'You speak English,' Lauren blurted out. 'Thank goodness.' A relieved sigh escaped her lips.

Alonso chuckled. 'My mother comes from Yorkshire and we lived there until I was ten. I also went to Leeds University. This is why I'm usually asked to deal with any overseas enquiries, especially those from English-speaking countries.'

'I can understand why. I'd been concerned about going into detail, but now it won't be an issue. Thanks for getting back to me so promptly, I really appreciate it.' Lauren motioned to Matt to take out his notebook. 'I'm going to put you on speaker because my detective sergeant, Matt Price, is here with me.'

'Good morning,' Matt said, leaning in slightly towards the phone.

'*Buenos días*,' the man replied. 'How can I help you exactly?'

'We're currently investigating several murders that we believe might link back to a case from the 1990s involving a Ronald Whitlock, who was extradited to Spain, tried for several murders, and incarcerated. We have recently learnt that Whitlock died in prison and we'd like to know more about the nature of his death, if you're able to assist?'

Alonso was silent and Lauren could hear typing. Was he pulling up the information for her?

'We do have strict protocols regarding what can be shared, however, in this instance I can inform you of what happened,' Alonso finally answered. 'Whitlock was found dead in his cell on the morning of 20 June.'

'Was there a note left beside the body?' Lauren asked, leaning forward slightly in her chair, wondering whether that could be their link.

'No.'

'Oh well, it was a thought. Please continue,' Lauren said, sitting back. She glanced over at Matt, who gave a slight shrug.

'Initially, suicide was suspected but following our investigation and the postmortem, it was later determined to be a suspicious death.'

Lauren's brow furrowed in thought as she absently tapped her pen on the desk. It certainly complicated things. 'Have you arrested anyone?'

'We have charged one of the other inmates,' Alonso said.

'Can you tell us exactly what happened?' Lauren asked, trying to piece together the events to see if they fitted in any way with theirs. She noticed Matt jotting down some notes out of the corner of her eye.

'When Whitlock was discovered, his wrist had been cut. He had bled out.'

'And what made you determine that it wasn't suicide?' Lauren asked, leaning forward again. Something wasn't adding up, but what?

'Several things. First of all, he was due to be released in a few years' time and also had a parole hearing coming up so he might have been out even sooner. What motive would there be for him to take his own life? As far as we were aware, there had been no significant changes in his personal life outside of the prison. Second, and more important, the pathologist believed it would have been impossible for Whitlock to have inflicted the wounds on himself. Whitlock was left-handed and it was his left wrist that was cut.'

'Couldn't he have used his right hand?' Matt asked, glancing up from his notes.

'This was discussed with the pathologist, but the cut was too clean, with no hesitation marks. Even if Whitlock was ambidextrous, it's unlikely he'd have been able to kill himself so easily.'

Lauren nodded thoughtfully, her mind whirring. She agreed that it was murder and not suicide. But why? What was the motive?

'How did you discover who committed the crime?' Matt asked.

'Cameras showed the last person entering Whitlock's cell before lights were out. After killing him, the perpetrator placed Whitlock on the bed and covered him, so it wasn't discovered until the next morning that he was dead. After many hours of questioning, the inmate finally admitted to the murder.'

'Was he asked why he did it?' Matt asked, jotting down more notes.

'Yes. He told the investigating officers it was because Whit-lock had threatened him.'

'Threatened him over what?' Lauren asked, her eyebrows raised sceptically. That explanation sounded a little too neat and tidy to her.

Alonso paused. 'According to the statement I have in front of me, he didn't say. It's not unusual for there to be fights in prison over what, to the rest of us, seems unimportant.'

'That sort of makes sense. What can you tell us about this inmate?' Lauren asked. She still wasn't buying the threat motive, but she let it go for now.

'He's sixty-five and in prison for a triple murder. He won't be released in his lifetime.'

'So, basically, there's going to be no comeback on this man because he has no chance of getting out of prison anyway?' Matt clarified, sharing a concerned glance with Lauren, and shaking his head.

'Unfortunately, yes, that is correct. Although he will lose many of his privileges.'

'Like?' Matt asked.

'Using the computers. Workshops. Social events that we hold in the prison,' Alonso said.

Lauren sat back in her chair, chewing her lower lip pensively. She didn't buy that it was simply over being threat-ened. It sounded too easy. There had to be some other explana-tion. The murderer would have had to have been given an incentive. Although the privileges didn't seem much to them, she suspected that inside it would be a different matter. Had he been paid? Or maybe one of his family members had been threatened or offered something in exchange for him commit-ting the murder?

'Is it possible for us to interview this inmate?' Lauren asked, deciding to follow up on her hunch.

'Maybe, but he doesn't speak English.'

'Could we interview him with an interpreter? You would be perfect,' Lauren suggested. She shared another glance with Matt, who nodded his agreement.

'Leave it with me and I will speak to the prison warden. It's not my decision to make,' Alonso said.

'Thanks. We could do it via Zoom. Could you tell us what's happened to Whitlock's body?'

'Following the postmortem, it was released to his family.'

'Do you have the family's details?' Lauren asked. They should follow up on that lead as well.

'It doesn't appear to be on the file that I have in front of me.'

'Has the funeral taken place?' Matt asked.

'Yes. According to the notes it took place here in Spain, not far from the prison.'

'I see. Well, thank you very much for your help, Mr Alonso.' Lauren beamed, even though he couldn't see it.

'Please call me Manuel.'

'Thank you, Manuel, you've greatly assisted us. We'll wait to hear from you regarding interviewing the inmate. The sooner the better, please.' Lauren's tone was polite but her words carried an undercurrent of determination. She wouldn't let this drop until she got to the bottom of what really happened, especially if it had a bearing on their case.

'Of course. I'll be in touch again soon.'

Lauren ended the call and turned to Matt. 'So what do you think? Something doesn't add up here.'

Matt nodded in agreement. 'Definitely. We need to talk to that inmate to see what he knows.'

'Agreed. We also need to track down Whitlock's family,' she said, making a mental list of their next steps.

'Ma'am, if the funeral took place in Spain, then they may well be living over there.'

Lauren nodded. 'Ellie will be crucial here. We'll ask her to track down the family. And we need to get back to the chief constable today, if possible. He could be at risk, along with the other people working at Camborne during that time.'

'I imagine the people overseas will be safer. So we're left with the chief constable and the other remaining person,' Matt said.

'You're right. We need to impress on the chief constable that it's imperative he's totally honest with us regarding the whole operation,' Lauren added. 'And not hold back like we thought he was.'

'Yes, ma'am. I agree, but whether he'll tell us everything remains to be seen. He might want to cover his back in case there's a chance something will come back on him. To protect his position.'

Matt's observation was sharp, and Lauren appreciated his insight. It echoed her own concerns about the challenges they faced, not only from the investigation itself, but from the intricate web of allegiances and secrets within the force.

'You're right. I'll contact his office and make us an appointment for later today. If I stress the urgency, he might agree to see us.'

Matt left the office and Lauren leant back in her chair, her attention drifting momentarily to the window. At least now they had a path forward, even if it was fraught with uncertainty and potential danger. *One step at a time*, she reminded herself, turning her attention back to the room, ready to tackle the next phase of their investigation.

'Ma'am,' Matt said, putting his head around her door.

Lauren looked up from her computer screen, tired from staring at the mounting emails in her inbox. 'What is it?'

'Nancy Swift, the officer from Camborne, has been tracked down. She's living a couple of hours away from here in Okehampton, West Devon, and uses her married name of Lawson which is why Ellie couldn't find her initially. She's now divorced and lives alone. We need to discuss what to do next.'

Lauren's heart skipped a beat. Was this a breakthrough? A glimmer of hope sparked in her chest. 'That's excellent,' she said, her voice bright. 'I'll be out in a tick.'

'Great,' Matt said, before disappearing from the doorway.

She hurriedly finished the email she was in the middle of writing, her fingers flying across the keyboard. With a final click of the mouse, she pushed back her chair, and marched into the office, standing next to the whiteboard and noticing that Swift's location had already been added underneath her name.

Lauren crossed her arms and scanned the room. 'Attention,' she called out, making sure they were all listening. 'Nancy Swift needs to be warned of the situation.'

'Shall I speak to her on the phone?' Matt asked, already reaching for the receiver on his desk.

'No,' Lauren said firmly, shaking her head. 'This needs to be done in person. We can't risk any miscommunication or have her brush it off as a prank call.'

Clem leant forward in his chair, appearing concerned. 'Should we offer her protection?'

'Yes, most definitely,' Lauren said, without hesitation. 'We need to get onto that immediately. Jenna, see if you can find a safe house close by that we can use,' she commanded, leaving no room for debate.

Jenna nodded, her fingers already typing away at her keyboard. 'Yes, ma'am. When you say close by, do you have somewhere in mind?'

'Within ten miles,' Lauren replied. 'Otherwise, every time we need to interview her it will take too much time out of our day and we can't afford to waste a single minute.'

'Consider it done,' Jenna said, jotting something down on the notebook that was on her desk.

Lauren turned to face Clem, who had a pensive expression on his face. 'How are we on the CCTV, Clem?' she asked, her voice tight with anticipation.

Clem ran a hand through his hair. 'We've checked out the cameras leading to the three victims' places. Nothing actually stands out, ma'am. No cars that are similar,' he responded, with a frustrated sigh.

Jenna looked up from her screen, her eyes narrowed in thought. 'Well, if the victims were expertly targeted, then perhaps they used different cars each time so we couldn't trace them.' She tapped her pen against her chin. 'It's what I'd do. It's pretty basic stuff.'

Lauren nodded, a grim expression on her face. 'Yes, you're right. We do seem to be dealing with an expert. What about the knives? Any luck on finding where they were purchased?' She glanced at Billy, her eyebrow raised in anticipation of his response.

'Yes,' the officer said, his voice tinged with satisfaction. 'I contacted the stores who sell knives within the Devon and Cornwall district, and one in Plymouth reported selling five of a similar description to the murder weapons, in a single purchase a little over two weeks ago.'

A surge of adrenaline coursed through Lauren. Now they were getting somewhere. They might be dealing with a professional, but that didn't make them impossible to catch.

'Fantastic. Any details on the person who bought them?' Lauren asked, hoping that they'd used a traceable credit card.

'Unfortunately not, ma'am, because they paid by cash. I asked the manager about CCTV footage and she's agreed to check if they still have it. Usually it's only kept for two weeks.'

Lauren's jaw clenched and a flicker of annoyance whipped through her. How could they not know whether or not they still had the footage? 'Well let's hope they can find it.'

'Yes, ma'am. I also asked if anyone would remember the purchase but the manager thought it unlikely because it was made on a Saturday when they're busy. I want to visit the shop and ask around, anyway. Five knives is a lot. One of the staff might remember. I also want to check the CCTV footage in person in case they still have it. I know it's a two-hour drive but I think it's worth it. Is that okay?'

'Yes, it's a good idea. You can go now,' Lauren agreed, impressed that Billy was taking the initiative.

'I thought on my way home I'd go to Truro hospital to visit Tamsin. She's been texting me how bored she is with not being able to do anything.'

'Buy her a basket of fruit,' Matt suggested. 'I'll give you some money.'

'Me, too,' Jenna said, reaching for her bag.

'Count me in,' Clem added, pulling out his wallet.

'And me,' Ellie said, picking up her purse from the desk.

Lauren pulled out five pounds from her pocket and gave it to Billy. 'This is all the cash I have. Is that enough?'

'Yeah. If we all chip in five pounds that will be thirty. I can get some of her favourite chocolates, too. Thanks, you lot. She'll be stoked.'

Lauren waited until the money had been passed over to Billy before continuing. 'Okay, now we know that five knives have been bought, I think we can assume the killer intends there to be five victims, not ten, even though they're using the "Ten Green Bottles" song,' Lauren said, tapping her fingers on the desk she was standing beside, her mind working overtime.

'In which case, ma'am, the other two victims are likely to be Nancy Lawson, and the chief constable. That makes sense because they don't have access to the others that are overseas or to the ones who've died. It's something we need to look into,' Matt said with urgency.

'Yes. That's right,' Lauren confirmed.

'Another thing, ma'am,' Clem said, raising his hand slightly to catch Lauren's attention.

She turned to him, frowning slightly. 'Yes?'

'If we're using Ellie and it's taken her a while to ascertain who the potential victims are and where they live, then how come the murderer knows?' the officer said, his tone serious and slightly puzzled.

'What are you saying exactly?' Lauren asked, cautiously processing the implications of his comment.

Clem sucked in a deep breath, staring directly at Lauren. 'Do you think that someone in the force is feeding them the information?'

A chill ran down Lauren's spine at the thought, but she quickly pushed it aside. She shook her head slowly. 'That's a big leap to make. If the killer already knows the Camborne officers' names, then they could do their own research to locate them.'

'But the fact that they only bought five knives, implies that they knew in advance where everyone was,' Clem countered, his voice insistent.

Was he right? Her heart sank at the prospect. If that was the case, then the investigation had now got a whole lot harder. But she didn't buy it. Not yet. They would need more proof.

'It's a possibility but I'm not sure,' she said, deliberately keeping her tone measured. 'All the information is out there if you know where to look. Ellie, did you use a police database to discover the whereabouts of the ex-Camborne officers?'

Ellie shook her head, her expression thoughtful. 'I used a mix of police and regular databases, some of which aren't readily accessible unless you know where to look.'

'Would it be easy for someone to access these details?'

'I wouldn't say easy, but it's possible. But you'd certainly need to know the names of people to look for. I used police HR records to work out who worked at Camborne during the 1990s – although the recording systems weren't like they are now.'

Lauren's thoughts returned to what Clem had suggested. What if the murderer was someone they knew? Her insides clenched at the thought, but she couldn't dismiss it entirely. It would certainly explain how the killer was able to get away with what they had. But... it was too early to start accusing anyone.

'I see. Well, it's something to bear in mind but we can't make any rash accusations. I want to give you all a quick update on my side of things.' She stood against the edge of the desk and met the eyes of her team members one by one, ensuring she had their full attention. 'I've requested an interview with the man who killed Whitlock, and I'm waiting for confirmation. We'll need an interpreter.' As she spoke, her fingers traced the edge of the desk, betraying a hint of the underlying tension she felt about the delicate nature of these negotiations. 'I've also had confirmation that we can interview the chief constable again. Matt and I will be doing that. He needs to be warned.' She might have sounded in control but internally she was all over the place. She doubted the chief constable was going to be receptive to her suggestion that he go into a safe house.

'What about visiting Nancy Lawson?' Jenna asked.

'I was coming to that. We'll head straight there from Exeter, after interviewing the chief constable,' she explained, already planning the logistics of the trip.

'Couldn't one of us go?' Jenna suggested.

Lauren paused, considering her words. It sort of made sense, but she'd rather go herself, with Matt. She shook her head firmly. 'No, Matt and I will go. Okehampton is much closer to Exeter than Penzance. But contact Okehampton station and ask them to keep an eye on her property until we arrive.'

TWENTY-TWO
WEDNESDAY, 17 JULY

Matt and Lauren were shown into Chief Constable Warren Johnson's office by his assistant. He was sitting behind his desk with an impatient look on his face. Matt glanced at photographs on the wall of him standing with other officers and a number of famous people – royalty, politicians, and other celebrities. Was that all the chief constable did now: glad-handing with the rich and famous? Matt would hate that. He loved the day-to-day police work that involved catching criminals. Whitney and Leigh had wanted him to go for his inspectors' exam and he'd considered it. But now he was glad he hadn't. Admin wasn't his forte and nor was working out budgets... Well, he assumed it wasn't. He hadn't actually done that, other than their household expenses.

'I don't have long,' the chief constable said, gesturing to the two chairs in front of his desk. 'Please sit.' His body language conveyed a sense of urgency that was different from the last time they'd sat around the table, even though then he'd also had to leave promptly.

Why was he acting differently? Did he know more than he was letting on?

'Thank you, sir,' Lauren said, dropping down on one of the chairs, leaving Matt to sit on the other.

'What's the problem, DI Pengelly,' the chief constable asked, leaning back in his chair, and staring at them both, a condescending look in his eye.

Did he think they were wasting his time, or was it a tactic to intimidate them?

'We've now had three people murdered, and we're concerned that this is related to an operation that took place in 1997 when you were DCI at Camborne, sir,' Lauren said, clinically. 'There were ten officers involved in the case. Three are now dead, having been murdered. Additionally, three had already died. Two are living overseas and that leaves you and Nancy Lawson, who was known as Nancy Swift when you worked there. We're obviously concerned that you both might be at risk.'

Matt scrutinised the chief constable's face for his reaction. But he wasn't giving anything away. His features remained impassive.

'I see. And you're convinced that I'm next on the list, are you?'

'It's looking that way, sir,' Lauren said.

'Don't worry about me.' His tone was nonchalant, but his eyes momentarily flickered to the door. 'I have security. Whoever the killer is, they won't be able to access me easily. I suggest you focus your attention on the other potential victim.'

'Nancy Lawson. Do you remember her, sir?' Lauren asked.

Good question, considering he was extremely vague about the other victims when they last spoke to him.

Chief Constable Johnson rested his arms on the table and glanced up. Body language indicating thought, but he'd know that and it could be for effect.

'I believe so. Red hair?'

'I don't know, sir,' Lauren said.

'Do you have security twenty-four seven?' Matt asked, trying to gauge the level of protection the chief constable had.

'They're with me for a significant amount of time, but I can increase the security detail around my house if that's what's necessary. How far are you into the investigation? Do you have a suspect – or suspects?'

Lauren adjusted her posture, until she was more upright in the chair. 'As I mentioned, it's linked to an operation that took place in the 1990s involving Ronald Whitlock, who was hiding in Cornwall. He was extradited to Spain and found guilty of several counts of murder. He—'

'Yes, I remember the case. Being part of it was instrumental in my promotion. But that all took place over twenty-five years ago... almost thirty. Are you sure it's to do with these recent murders? What's happened to make it so?' He frowned.

'Whitlock was recently murdered in a Spanish prison. I've been discussing this with a contact I have over there and hope to interview the murderer.'

'Good work,' he said, nodding approvingly. But his jaw had tightened. Was he now considering the threat real? 'Do you have any idea, though, why his death has been instrumental in these current murders?'

'We're working on it,' Lauren said. 'What can you tell us about the operation, sir?'

The chief constable moved awkwardly in his leather swivel chair, his arms folded across his chest. What was he hiding?

'My memory is sketchy but from what I remember, Whitlock was being shielded by someone in Cornwall, close to Camborne. My boss received a tip-off from the Met regarding Whitlock being here under an assumed name, and we undertook an investigation to locate him. An early morning sweep was undertaken on the property where Whitlock was staying, which was a large house on the outskirts of Camborne, owned by a millionaire. Whitlock was arrested and extradited to Spain. That's as far as Camborne CID's involvement went.'

'What about the millionaire who was shielding him?' Matt asked.

'His name escapes me. But he, too, was arrested, charged, and went to prison. I'm sure you can find the details.'

'Why didn't you tell us about this case at our previous interview?' She sounded calm, but her annoyance was given away by the tight lines around her mouth. Although Matt suspected the chief constable wouldn't notice.

He didn't blame Lauren being angry. Knowing sooner might have led to them preventing Craig Garland's death.

'I'd forgotten about it,' he replied without missing a beat. But the response was a bit quick for Matt's liking, as if he'd already planned it.

The longer the interview progressed, the more Matt suspected that the chief constable knew more than he was letting on. An operation of that scale, involving international extradition and collaboration with the Met, seemed too significant to simply forget. Was there more to the story than the chief constable was letting on? Had he deliberately withheld details? In which case, why?

'How could you have forgotten? It was a big operation and, as you told us, was instrumental in your career,' Lauren pressed.

Chief Constable Johnson's face darkened, and he leant forward slightly. 'Because it slipped my mind. Now, is there anything else?' He drummed his fingers impatiently on the desk.

Lauren quickly glanced at Matt, who was clearly frustrated.

'Well, I would like to reiterate, sir, that your life could be in danger. I suggest you increase your security detail until we arrest the person, or persons, responsible. After leaving here we'll be visiting Nancy Lawson and will suggest that she goes into the safe house we've arranged for her. Would you consider that at all?'

'Absolutely not,' the chief constable said with a huff. He glanced at his watch, a subtle indication of his growing impatience – or perhaps a desire to deflect from the topic at hand. 'Now, I really have another meeting to attend. I can assure you that I'll be fine. You need to get on with finding the murderer and stop wasting time on me.'

'Before we leave, sir, do you have any ideas yourself as to why this is happening now and who might be responsible?' Matt asked, deciding to risk probing further because it was unlikely that they'd be given another chance.

'From what you've said, I imagine it's something to do with Whitlock.'

'So what are you thinking? That he was murdered, and now they're coming after all the officers involved in the original arrest?'

Matt sensed Lauren was watching him. Was she okay with him suddenly coming forward like this? She no doubt would let her feelings be known once they'd left.

'I've no idea,' the chief constable said, banging his fist on his desk. 'You're wasting time talking to me. I've told you everything I know.' His tone indicated finality.

'Okay, thank you, sir,' Lauren said, signalling the end of their questioning.

Matt sucked in a breath. The chief constable's body language and responses were a mix of dismissive and evasive and Matt was distrustful of the man's claim of ignorance, especially given someone as pivotal as Whitlock was in his career. The quick glance at his watch, the abrupt dismissal of their concerns, and his insistence on their departure didn't sit right with Matt. Had their visit stirred something that Chief Constable Johnson wished to keep buried? Was his nonchalance a facade meant to deter further enquiry? The conversation, rather than providing answers, seemed to deepen the mystery and urgency of their investigation.

As they left the office and headed down the corridor towards the station exit, Lauren turned to Matt. 'Wow... I didn't expect that of you.'

'I'm sorry, I knew that if the questions weren't posed now then we might not get the chance again. I'm sorry if you thought I'd overstepped the mark.'

'No need to apologise. You were right to ask. What's your view of his responses?' she asked.

Matt pondered for a moment, his steps slowing as he weighed his words carefully. 'I think it's very strange that he's not worried at all about his security. And yes, he can up his security, but it seems as if he knows that he's okay. It's a bit dodgy, if you ask me.'

'So, what you're saying is, if he's convinced that he's okay, then he might be a part of this?' Lauren's forehead creased.

'Maybe...'

'That's a strong accusation,' Lauren said, echoing his thoughts, but not appearing to disbelieve him.

'I know, ma'am, but that's only between you and me. Obviously, we can't do anything about it until we have some irrefutable proof,' Matt said with a sigh. 'But didn't you think it was odd the way he dismissed it? He didn't seem at all concerned that he could be the target of a successful murderer. We've had three ex-officers killed so far, and yet he doesn't seem at all bothered.'

'I agree with you, but it could be his arrogance,' Lauren said, staring directly at him. 'Think about it this way. If the chief constable was part of these murders, then surely he would be acting more concerned, because he'd know that's how we'd expect him to be? Do you understand what I mean?'

Matt slowly nodded. Put like that then Lauren could be correct and he was letting his imagination run away with him.

'Yes, that's a good point, ma'am. Unless he was operating a double bluff...' Or was he going too far? 'Anyway, we should know more once we discover why Whitlock was murdered. Hopefully then we should be able to connect the dots.'

'Agreed. But for now, we need to visit Nancy Lawson.'

As they walked back to Lauren's car, Matt couldn't shake the feeling that they were missing a crucial piece of the puzzle – a key that would unlock the motivations behind these targeted killings – and that the chief constable was somehow involved.

Lauren pulled up outside the cream semi-detached, modern property in a quiet, residential neighbourhood of Okehampton where Nancy Lawson lived. The area exuded an air of tranquillity, a stark contrast to the tension which was Lauren's constant companion. There was no police presence – had anyone been keeping an eye on the property as she'd requested?

Two cars were parked side by side on the drive, and the curtains to the house were drawn.

Lauren frowned as she turned to Matt. 'It's odd that the curtains are closed at this time of day,' she said, her voice low and cautious. 'Could someone be there?' Her fingers tapped nervously against the steering wheel, as unease settled in her gut.

She looked back at the house, taking in the closed-off facade. A knot of apprehension formed in her stomach, twisting and tightening with each passing second. Something wasn't right. There was danger behind the drawn curtains, she knew it.

'Yes, ma'am. We should be very careful. I'll call in the number plates of the two cars before we make a move.' Matt pulled out his phone with a determined gesture, his jaw set.

Lauren nodded, her lips pressed together in a tight line. She waited while Matt called, her heart pounding in her chest as he put the phone on speaker.

'Hi, Clem, it's Matt. Can you run two plates for me, please? We'll stay on the line whilst you do it,' Matt urgently requested.

'No problem, Sarge,' Clem replied, the sound of typing audible in the background.

Matt's eyes never left the house as he called out the details, his vigilance unwavering, and they sat in silence waiting for Clem to feed back to them.

'Sarge,' Clem called out after a couple of minutes, his voice breaking the tense silence. 'The first number you gave me belongs to Nancy Lawson.'

'Yeah, that's expected,' Matt said, with a nod, his expression grim.

'And the other one's from a stolen car, reported missing this morning.'

Lauren's stomach dropped, a cold dread seeping through her veins. Was the murderer in the house? Were they too late to save her? Thoughts ricocheted around her head, each one more terrifying than the last.

'Thanks, Clem. Contact Okehampton station and ask for backup to be sent to Nancy Lawson's house, pronto,' Matt said, a new edge of resolve in his voice. He ended the call and turned to Lauren. 'Shall we wait for backup or check out what's going on? Her life could be in danger.'

Lauren swallowed hard, her mouth dry. 'We can't wait,' she said, determination and fear coursing through her at the same time. 'If the curtains are drawn it means that whoever's in there can't see out. Let's have a look around the house, see if we can see anything.'

They left the car and hurried down the drive in silence. The tension in the air was palpable, each step towards the back of the house fraught with uncertainty and danger. Lauren's heart raced, her senses heightened and alert.

They reached the rear of the house, and she immediately noticed that the curtains covering the French doors hadn't been drawn, presumably because they faced the garden which provided privacy from prying eyes.

Matt took a cautious step forward and leant in slightly to get a better view. He quickly returned to Lauren, a look of horror etched on his face. 'Nancy's holding up a chair, trying to fight a man off. We need to get in there straight away,' he whispered in a strained voice.

Lauren swallowed hard at the thought of the woman inside, fighting for her life. The urgency of the situation left no room for hesitation. 'Yes,' she said firmly, despite the fear gripping her chest.

'I'll try the door and see if it's open. We can't wait for backup or she might end up dead,' Matt said.

They approached the French doors and Matt turned the handle. To their surprise, it was unlocked.

They burst into the room. 'Police! Stop what you're doing,' Matt shouted.

The intruder, a man wielding a knife, turned towards them, his expression a mix of shock and defiance. 'Go away!' he shouted, but his threat was cut short as Nancy hit him over the head with the chair.

The impact stunned the man momentarily, giving Matt the opportunity to rush forward and tackle him to the ground.

The knife went flying across the room.

Matt pulled out handcuffs from his pocket.

'I'm arresting you on suspicion of attempted murder. You do not have to say anything. But it may harm your defence if you do not mention when questioned something which you later rely on in court. Anything you do say may be given in evidence,'

Matt recited calmly, leaving no doubt as to who had the upper hand.

Lauren let out a shaky breath, relief washing over her as she watched Matt secure the suspect. They'd made it in time, but the knowledge of how close they'd come to another tragedy twisted her stomach in knots. She turned to Nancy. 'Are you okay?' she asked gently, ready to offer whatever support she could.

'Yes,' the woman replied, still catching her breath. Her hands shook. The result of the ordeal, no doubt. 'I'm surprised I was able to fight him off. Adrenaline shot through me, giving extra energy.'

'Well thank goodness for that,' Lauren said, her voice laced with admiration and relief. Nancy was one brave woman, managing to defend herself until help arrived.

Lauren pulled on some disposable gloves and picked up the knife. She turned to the man in handcuffs and spotted something peeping out of his back pocket. She grabbed it, her eyes widening as she realised it was a note with *Seven Green Bottles* written on it. She dropped the evidence into a bag while processing the implications of this discovery.

She turned back to Nancy to make sure she was still okay. As they spoke, the distant sound of sirens grew louder until it culminated in the flashing lights of police cars pulling up to the house.

The moment the reinforcements arrived, the tension in the room began to dissipate. 'We've got it from here,' one of the officers said as they took hold of the handcuffed intruder.

'You know, I had requested that the house be put under observation,' Lauren said to the officer, despite realising that as a constable it wouldn't have been his responsibility.

'Yes, ma'am. We did have someone making a regular stop but they were called away following a nasty farming accident.'

'This could have turned out very nasty, too, if we hadn't

turned up,' Lauren snapped. 'Right, I want him taken to Penzance station because we'll be interviewing him there.'

'Yes, ma'am,' the officer said.

A mix of relief and exhaustion washed over Lauren. The fear that had gripped her heart only moments ago was now replaced with a deep sense of gratitude for their timely intervention and the bravery displayed by Nancy.

'What's your name?' Lauren asked the prisoner.

'Kevin Dixon and that's all you're getting out of me. However hard you try. And, by the way, I need a doctor,' he said, unsteady on his feet.

Was he making it up? Lauren couldn't take the risk. He might have injured himself when Matt tackled him to the ground.

'That can be arranged,' she said, coldly, as she assessed his condition and not seeing anything untoward. Nevertheless, they would follow procedure and give him the medical attention he'd requested.

After Dixon was taken away, Lauren turned back to Nancy. 'We'll need you to come down to the station to make a statement. Did he say anything? Can you remember exactly what happened?' Her questions were gentle, aiming to piece together the sequence of events without being overwhelming.

Nancy nodded, taking a moment to collect her thoughts before responding. 'Yes. The doorbell went and I answered it because I was expecting a delivery. And he... he pushed his way in, grabbed my arm, drew the curtains, and pulled out a knife.'

A cold shiver ran down Lauren's spine as she imagined the scene. 'What did you do?' she enquired.

'I ran to the back of the room because I wanted to get away from him. Then he came for me, so I grabbed a chair, and a little while later you turned up.' Nancy's recounting of the events was fragmented, the shock clearly still fresh in her mind.

'Did he tell you why he was there?'

'He said it wasn't personal and that he had a job to do.'

'What do you think he meant by that?' Lauren asked, her eyebrows bunched up as she tried to make sense of the cryptic statement.

'I don't know. But he's not well. He was right when he said that to you.'

'Why do you think that?'

'Because when he pushed me inside, he sort of stopped to catch his breath and that's when I ran into the dining area and grabbed a chair to protect myself.'

'Why didn't you go to the French windows and run outside?' Lauren pressed, trying to understand Nancy's thinking in the moment.

'I don't know, I wasn't thinking straight. I was looking for a weapon of some sort to fight him off.' Nancy's voice shook and she looked down at her hands which were also trembling. She was clearly more shaken than she was letting on.

'Then what happened?' Lauren asked softly.

'While I was waving the chair, I said if it isn't personal then why do it? He said it was for the money. Then he started to cough and I made a dash for the door but he came back at me again. Then you appeared.'

Lauren processed Nancy's words, trying to figure out the motive behind the attack. 'You did a good job, so well done,' she said, wanting to reassure the woman.

But inside Lauren wasn't so reassured. What if they'd arrived a few minutes later? They could've been faced with another body. And the killer could have escaped and gone after the chief constable. That reminded her.

'Did he say anything about the chief constable. Warren Johnson?'

Nancy frowned. 'You mean Johnson who was the DCI at Camborne when I worked there?'

'Yes. Him,' Lauren said.

'That bastard,' Nancy spat, her face twisting with anger.

'Why do you say that?' Lauren asked, taken aback by the venom in the woman's voice.

'Nothing. It doesn't matter now. It all happened many years ago. Why did you ask if my attacker mentioned him? He didn't.'

'We're investigating three murders linked to when you worked at Camborne on the Whitlock case. It led us to believe that you and the chief constable might be in danger.'

'Oh.' Nancy sank into a chair, and let out a sigh. 'Well, thanks for getting here in time. But the Whitlock case was years ago. Why come for us now?'

'Whitlock was murdered in a Spanish jail and we believe it might be linked to that. I'm hoping that Dixon will give us the details. Returning to the chief constable, why didn't you like him?' Lauren asked, more for curiosity's sake than believing it related to the investigation.

'I'd no idea he'd risen to that rank. I left the station not long after working on the Whitlock case. I hated working for him. He was a two-faced creep. He didn't like me either.'

'Were you one of the women who complained about his inappropriate behaviour?'

That could certainly be behind her dislike of him.

'No. That happened after the Whitlock case. If I'd have been there, then I would have added my complaint, too. Although it was all dusted under the carpet... so my friend told me. But that's what happened back then.'

'What did you do after leaving the force?' Lauren asked, wanting a clearer picture of the woman's life.

'I went into business with my husband. We opened a small nursery, selling exotic plants. After we divorced, I took over the business and sold it last year when I retired.'

Lauren nodded, taking in the new information. There was

definitely more to the case than met the eye. The attack on Nancy, the murders and the connections to the past all swirled in her mind, forming a complex web that needed untangling.

TWENTY-FOUR
WEDNESDAY, 17 JULY

'Ma'am, you are not going to like this,' Clem called out the moment Lauren marched back into the office ready to get the team working on bringing the disparate parts of the case together.

'What is it?' she asked, coming to an immediate stop in front of the officer's desk, with Matt close behind.

'Kevin Dixon's been taken to the hospital so won't be here for you to interview.'

'Do we know why?' she asked, her eyebrows knitting together. 'He didn't appear to be injured in the scuffle. When we arrested him, he mentioned needing a doctor, but I didn't believe him.'

'It's something else, but I don't know what. The custody sergeant called the doctor, I believe. I'll see if I can find out what's wrong with him,' Clem said, lifting the handset from the phone on his desk.

'Nancy Lawson said she thought he wasn't well,' Matt reminded her.

'Okay, we'll either interview him at the hospital or, if they don't keep him in, wait for him to be brought back here,' Lauren said, internally weighing up her options.

Her phone rang and, pulling it out of her pocket, she glanced down at the screen. It was an international number.

'Pengelly.'

'This is Manuel Alonso.'

Good. She'd been hoping to hear from him today.

'Hello, Manuel. Have you arranged my interview with Whitlock's killer?'

'Ummm... no.' Manuel hesitated. 'He's refusing to speak to you.'

'What?' she said, her voice sharp. She hadn't expected that. 'Surely you can persuade him. It's important to my investigation.' She exchanged a glance with Matt and shook her head.

'It doesn't work like that, I'm afraid. He has to agree to the interview and, currently, he's refusing to speak. He's in solitary confinement and won't answer any questions from anyone. If anything changes, you'll be the first to know. I'm sorry I don't have better news for you.'

Not as sorry as she was.

'Thanks for trying,' she said, a sigh escaping her lips.

'Bad news?' Matt asked as she ended the call.

'Whitlock's murderer refuses to speak to anyone. So that puts paid to our interview with him.'

'We might not need him, now,' Matt said with a conciliatory shrug.

'True...' Lauren turned to address the team. 'Right... our suspect's in hospital, and Whitlock's murderer is refusing to speak to me.' She glanced at her watch. It was already nearly seven and they'd come to a standstill. 'I suggest we all go home, as it's getting late, and reconvene first thing tomorrow. One way or another, Kevin Dixon will be interviewed in the morning, either at the hospital or here, and we'll find out the truth.'

* * *

Matt glanced in Lauren's direction as she drove them to the hospital. With pursed lips and a steely stare, she concentrated on the road ahead. On arriving that morning, they'd learnt that Dixon had terminal cancer, which meant it was doubtful he'd be prosecuted because he wouldn't be alive by the time the case reached court.

'You okay, ma'am?' he asked.

'Yes,' she replied, staring straight ahead. 'I was running through what's on the line here. If Kevin Dixon refuses to speak, like Whitlock's killer, then we're left with no leads at all. I'm convinced someone is pulling the strings, or why would he have told Nancy Lawson that it wasn't personal and just a job. But who? And more to the point, why?'

'Dixon has nothing to gain by keeping quiet because he'll end up spending the remainder of his life in custody. Anyway, we're jumping the gun here. He might be prepared to talk,' Matt said, crossing his fingers and holding it up for her to see.

'When we arrested him, he said all we were going to learn from him was his name,' Lauren said, tapping her fingers on the steering wheel.

'Yeah, but he won't be the first to say that, or the last. Maybe we can *persuade* him to talk,' Matt said, doing quote marks with his fingers.

'What do you have in mind?' Lauren asked, arching an eyebrow.

'Tell him we'll speak to the Crown Prosecution Service and ask them to suggest home detention for the rest of his life. At least then he can spend some quality time with his family. Surely that would be an enticement.'

'If he has a family to spend time with? It could be that he's not only being paid to carry out the murders but also to not disclose anything, if caught. He could be doing that for his family, too. In which case he's not going to help us.' Lauren shook her head, her expression sceptical.

'I'll ask Ellie to look into his wider background,' Matt said, pulling out his phone and pressing the shortcut key, his fingers moving swiftly over the screen.

'Hello, Matt.'

'Hey, Ellie, we're on the way to the hospital to see Dixon. We need something on him. Leverage to make him talk. Find out if he's got any family. If there's any money that's changed hands. Anything that might help.'

'Leave it with me,' Ellie said.

The ward where Dixon was being held was noisy with the sounds of the hospital staff going about their duties. When they reached his room, Lauren nodded at the officer on duty, who stepped to the side to allow them to enter. Dixon was on his own, handcuffed to the bed. A single window lit up the room, which was bare, with no personal possessions on show. Matt sucked in a breath, hoping that they'd get the information they needed from the man, who stared up at them nonchalantly.

'Good morning,' Lauren said. 'We're here to interview you regarding the murders of Carmel Driscoll, Jayne Freeman and Craig Garland, and the attempted murder of Nancy Lawson. This will be recorded,' she stated, hitting the record button on her phone, and placing it on the table. She pulled over one of the chairs that was situated by the wall and sat down. Matt did the same. 'Interview on 18 July. Those present: DI Pengelly, DS Price, and... please state your name for the recording.'

'Kevin Walter Dixon,' the man said, with a hint of defiance.

'How are you?' Lauren asked.

'Fine. They wanted to keep me in a bit longer after the battering you gave me,' he said, glaring at Matt.

Irritation at the accusation coursed through Matt but he

forced himself to remain composed. 'I'd hardly call it a *battering*. I pulled you to the floor to stop you from murdering Nancy Lawson.'

'Well, yeah, okay,' Dixon conceded.

'You don't seem at all bothered by it,' Matt added, noting the total lack of compassion in the man's voice.

'I'm going to die soon so no, I'm not.' Dixon slumped back in the bed, an air of resignation about him.

'Are you admitting to killing these people?' Matt asked, locking eyes with Dixon.

'Yes.'

'Why?' Matt asked.

'It was a job,' Dixon replied, as if the question was run of the mill.

'Who paid you to do it?' Lauren asked.

'No comment,' Dixon said, looking away.

'Have you always killed people for a living?' Matt pressed.

'No comment,' Dixon repeated, a blank expression on his face.

'Do you have a dog?' Lauren asked.

Dixon's mouth dropped open. 'Yeah...'

'An English Setter?'

'Why?' He frowned.

'Dog hairs were found on your first victim. So if you do try to retract your confession, we have evidence that you were with her.'

'I'm not planning to retract,' Dixon said, tension leaving his body.

'Did you send the threatening emails to each of the victims?' Matt asked.

'No,' Dixon said, shaking his head.

'You haven't requested a solicitor. Is there a reason for that?' Lauren asked, frowning.

'I don't need one. I've got six weeks left, maybe two months at the most. What's the point.' Dixon spread his hands out in front of him and stared at them.

Matt observed him closely, trying to find a crack in his demeanour, but the man's acceptance of his fate seemed to have built a wall around him that was hard to penetrate. Matt tapped his fingers on the armrest of the chair. This wasn't going well, and judging by the expression on Lauren's face she was feeling the same frustration.

His phone vibrated in his pocket and he checked the message. It was a text from Ellie. Dixon had a young daughter with cerebral palsy, and there had been recent deposits into an account, some of which had been used to pay for a new wheel-chair. He typed a quick *Thanks* back, before turning to the prisoner.

'I think I know the reason why you've done this,' Matt said, ensuring he sounded calm so as not to give away the flurry of activity in his mind.

'No, you don't,' Dixon retorted, his confidence appearing unshaken.

'You've got a daughter with cerebral palsy. Isobel.'

Dixon's jaw dropped in shock. 'How do you know that?' he asked, his voice fainter and not so confident.

'It doesn't matter how we know, but we do. And you've been paid a lot of money, some of which has been used for a new wheelchair, and I'm guessing much of the rest will be used for her continuing care,' Matt continued, observing the cracks showing in the man's facade.

'No comment,' Dixon said faintly, his voice lacking its previous defiance.

'Well, here's the thing,' Lauren added. 'You either tell us what we want to know, or that money will be taken as evidence, which means there'll be no support for your daughter once you've gone.'

'You can't do that,' Dixon said, his face a canvas of sheer terror.

'Oh yes, we can,' Lauren said.

'Look, if I tell you everything, you must promise that the money stays with my wife to look after Isobel.'

Matt glanced at the determined expression on Lauren's face. Surely she knew they couldn't make promises about the money. Okay, they needed the information, but messing with Dixon like that... that wasn't something he'd do.

'We'll do what we can,' Lauren said.

Good, she wasn't promising.

'What do you want to know?' Dixon said, his body slumped down into the bed.

'Let's start with who paid you and why?' Lauren said.

Dixon stared ahead for a while, until finally drawing in an audible breath. 'I received my instructions by letter sent to my home. It came from Ronnie Whitlock's girlfriend.'

'Ronnie Whitlock?' Matt repeated. 'As in the London gangster?'

'Yeah. That's him. His girlfriend's been paying me. She's been working with a police officer to find out where the victims live.'

'How do you know this?' Lauren said, exchanging a worried glance with Matt.

'Because she said so in the letter. This officer has always been involved with Whitlock and his gang.'

'You seem very well informed,' Matt said, frowning.

'This isn't my first rodeo, okay. I've known the gang for years and regularly worked for them.'

'Where's this letter?' Lauren asked.

'I destroyed it. That was why it was done in the old-fashioned way so nothing could be traced. We always work that way.'

'Who's the officer involved?' Lauren asked.

'I don't know.' Dixon glanced away. He was lying.

'Yes you do,' Matt said. 'Tell us.'

'I can't.'

'Then forget any deal to help your daughter,' Lauren said, waving a dismissive hand.

'If I tell you, my wife and daughter will need protection. I don't want anything coming back on them.'

'Okay, we can do that,' Lauren said.

'It's Warren Johnson.'

Matt's eyebrows shot up.

The chief constable.

'So, you're saying that Warren Johnson and Whitlock's girlfriend are in on this together. Why?' Lauren asked, her voice cold.

'Because the girlfriend had Whitlock's child, and he'd never been a part of his life. She was hoping that he'd be released soon, and now he's dead. She's holding everyone who put him there responsible. Johnson gave her details of all the officers involved and where they lived. These details were passed to me in the letter.'

Matt remained frozen to the spot, absorbing every word, aware of the implications of what they were being told.

'Why would Johnson do this?' Lauren asked.

'He was working with Whitlock at the time he was arrested and he's continued to provide information to Whitlock's gang in London. He also kept in touch with the girlfriend.'

'And who is this girlfriend?' Matt asked.

'I only know her as Mandy.'

'Where is she now?'

'Somewhere in London, I think, but I don't know exactly.'

'What about the cryptic notes you left. What's that all about?' Matt asked.

'I don't know. I was told to leave them. I didn't ask why. You now know everything, so what are you going to do?'

'You're still under arrest, but we'll speak to the Crown Prosecution Service and also find a safe place for your family,' Lauren said, with a promise of action.

Matt's heart went out to Dixon in a way, understanding his desperation to provide for his daughter. But the man was guilty of murder. Their next steps, however, were going to require careful execution.

TWENTY-FIVE
THURSDAY, 18 JULY

'Right, I want everyone to listen carefully, and this goes nowhere. Do you understand?' Lauren said, her voice serious as she gathered the whole team in the office. She scanned the room, ensuring everyone's attention was on her.

'Yes, ma'am,' they answered in unison, while exchanging puzzled glances with each other.

'As you're aware, we're back from interviewing the murderer, who has admitted the offences but... he has also made some very serious accusations.' She paused for a moment to allow her words to sink in. 'He maintains he was paid to do the job by Ronnie Whitlock's girlfriend, who was doing it as retaliation for his murder.'

'Why?' Clem asked.

'She has a child by him – well, not so much a child now. But this person hasn't met his father and now he never will. We don't know the reason behind Whitlock's murder but that aside, according to Dixon she was working with someone on the inside who provided her with the whereabouts of the victims and—'

'What the hell?' Billy interrupted, his mouth open.

'Do we know who?' Clem asked.

'Yes, if you let me continue,' Lauren said, her lips pressing into a thin line.

'Sorry, ma'am,' Clem said, glancing down at the floor.

Lauren cleared her throat. 'Dixon has implicated the chief constable.'

'You're kidding,' Billy said, his voice a mix of shock and disbelief.

'I wish I was,' Lauren said, with a sigh.

'First the sexual harassment accusations, and now this. What are we going to do?' Billy asked.

'Assuming that Dixon's telling us the truth, and we have no reason to believe he isn't, we have to decide how to play this. First of all, Ellie. I want you to find Whitlock's girlfriend. All we know is her name's Mandy.'

'Yes, ma'am,' Ellie said, reaching for her keyboard.

'Thanks. Next, I need to speak to the DCI regarding arresting the chief constable.'

'You're going to arrest him based solely on the word of the murderer?' Jenna asked, shaking her head slowly, appearing not to approve.

The officer was right. They should take their time and make sure everything added up because if they were wrong... she didn't even want to go there... But suffice to say, her career would come to a dramatic standstill – that was assuming she was even left with a job.

'No, I don't intend to be so rash, Jenna. What I should have said was *interview* him. But it will be with a view to an arrest if the circumstances warrant. It's not going to be an easy situation to navigate, whatever happens. I'm going to speak to the DCI now. Remember, this has to stay under wraps. I'll be back shortly.'

Lauren exited the room, her thoughts consumed with the task ahead and trusting that no one on the team was going to let her down by leaking the news. But they wouldn't. She was sure of it. They'd have nothing to gain by doing so.

When she reached DCI Mistry's office, she knocked on the door, holding her breath while waiting for a response. How on earth was she going to broach the issue with him without turning it into some sort of melodrama?

'Come in,' DCI Mistry called.

Her boss was sitting, as usual, with a pen in his hand and some folders on his desk in front of him. He was very much an administrative boss, not one to get involved in the day-to-day running of the team. For which she was immensely grateful. In his position she wouldn't be so relaxed.

'Sir, we've got an issue that needs dealing with urgently,' Lauren began, trying to gauge his reaction.

'What is it?' he enquired, setting his pen on the desk, and leaning back in his chair.

'We have arrested the killer, but he's informed us that he was paid to do the work by the girlfriend of Ronald Whitlock.'

'And the problem with this is?'

'She was able to give him information regarding the victims' whereabouts because a police officer told her,' Lauren explained, observing the DCI's body language closely. 'And... umm... this is the tricky bit. The officer who supposedly helped her was Chief Constable Johnson.'

DCI Mistry sat upright in his seat, his jaw set. 'Are you sure about this?'

'Not one hundred per cent, sir. We only have the word of Kevin Dixon, the murderer. At the moment we're tracking down the girlfriend to question her. But we certainly need to re-interview the chief constable and, considering we've already spoken to him twice, we need to be cautious. We don't want him to know that we suspect his involvement at this stage,' she said, the potential strategies and the risks they entailed at the forefront of her mind.

The DCI steepled his fingers and stared over Lauren's head for a few seconds.

Did he have a plan of action? Or was he going to leave it for Lauren to deal with? She wasn't sure what she wanted his response to be.

'Okay, Lauren,' he finally said, focusing on her. 'We need to tread very carefully because whatever we decide could have serious ramifications for all of us.'

You think?

'Yes, sir. Of course. What do you suggest?'

'We'll speak to the chief constable together. I'm going to phone for an appointment but keep it low key.' His tone was decisive, yet Lauren detected an undercurrent of concern as he picked up the phone and pressed a number.

'Hello, Val, it's DCI Mistry. I'd like an appointment to speak to the chief constable, please. Today.' A shadow crossed his face as he listened to the response. 'I see. Thank you. If you do hear from him, please let me know.' A crease formed between his brows as he finished the call. 'This isn't good.'

'What is it?' Lauren asked, her stomach in knots.

'It seems the chief constable has gone missing. He's missed two appointments this morning, and nobody can find him despite many attempts.'

This wasn't good.

'He must know we're onto him. Perhaps he's heard that we've arrested Dixon,' Lauren said, giving a frustrated sigh. 'What do you want to do now?'

Lauren's mind was already racing through the implications of his disappearance. None of which were sitting well. But it wasn't her decision to make. The DCI had to take the lead.

'Contact the control room and circulate a message to all units to see if he can be located.'

'Really, sir? Surely that would alert everyone on the force that something's wrong.'

'Not if it's worded in such a way that he's needed for an urgent meeting, or something that's not implicating him,' Mistry said.

'And you think I should do that, rather than you?' Lauren asked, surprised he didn't want to do it himself.

'Yes. Keep it within your team for now. I don't want to alert any of my staff that we have this issue.'

Or did he want to distance himself in case it all went pear-shaped? That wouldn't surprise her. He'd told her when she first arrived at Penzance that he was a career officer.

Now wasn't the time for Lauren to debate the DCI's motives.

'Okay, sir. Leave it with me. We'll also continue trying to locate Whitlock's girlfriend... There is something else that I haven't told you. I don't believe it's relevant to the murders but you should know.'

'What is it?' Mistry said, frowning.

'When working at Camborne, the chief constable was investigated for sexual harassment but the charges were dismissed because the evidence was deemed unreliable. Nancy Lawson, the final intended victim who we reached in time, commented on his behaviour when she worked at Camborne so I think he was lucky to have the charges dropped. He wouldn't be so lucky today.'

Mistry stared at her like a deer caught in the headlights. 'Anything else I'm not yet aware of?'

'No, sir. That's it.'

'Wow... this is one Thursday that I'm not going to forget.' He visibly pulled himself together. 'Thank you for the update, Lauren. Remember, this all requires the utmost discretion. I want to be kept informed every step of the way.'

She marched back to the main office, her steps echoing her urgency. Upon entering, the room went silent and the team stared at her, their faces etched with concern and anticipation.

'It turns out that Chief Constable Johnson has gone missing. Clem, I want you to contact comms and ask them to notify all units to be on the lookout for him. Don't say what it's for, but say he's urgently required,' Lauren commanded, her voice steady but her insides churning.

'Why do we have to do it?' Clem asked, with a frown.

'The DCI believes it's better coming from us.' She held up her hands in mock defeat. 'Don't ask,' she added, shaking her head to imply that she didn't understand it either.

'Okay, ma'am.' Clem picked up the phone and pressed one of the buttons, then sat waiting for it to be answered.

'Any luck in finding the girlfriend, Ellie?' Lauren asked, turning to the officer.

'No, sorry, not yet,' Ellie said, sounding frustrated.

'Right, let's check out CCTV and see if we can spot the chief constable. Find out the car he drives and get as close to his house as you can. Hopefully we can pick him up leaving this morning. Jenna and Clem, you do that. Billy and Ellie, continue looking into the chief constable. Look for anything that connects him to Whitlock, however small.'

Lauren retreated to her office, trying to gather her thoughts. None of this was rolling out as she'd imagined. Whatever the result of this investigation, nothing was going to be the same again. Guilty or otherwise, targeting Chief Constable Johnson was going to leave an indelible mark on the entire team and, she suspected, not in a good way. People wouldn't trust them again, even if they did solve the crime.

She glanced at the latest emails in her inbox, some of them sent in the middle of the night. What was it with some people? Didn't they realise that sending emails at that time was ridiculous? And it certainly didn't impress her. She sucked in a breath, about to tackle them when a knock on the door interrupted her and Matt walked in.

'I think we've located the chief constable. His car was

spotted at a service station about three miles from here,' Matt announced, sounding hopeful.

'That's fantastic. Come on, let's go. Before someone gives him the heads-up that we're looking for him. We'll take the team with us for backup.' A surge of adrenaline coursed through her as she stood up from her chair.

Lauren drove to the service station with Matt; and Jenna, Clem and Billy followed in a second car. Ellie was left in the office to coordinate their efforts. She parked near the window and took out her binoculars.

'I can see him on the left, he's with a woman,' she said, passing the binoculars to Matt.

'That's the girlfriend, Mandy Wilde,' Matt said, showing Lauren a photo of the attractive woman with short dark hair on his phone. 'Ellie's texted me this. She managed to locate the woman.'

'Excellent. Let's see him try and wriggle his way out of this. You and I will go in but play it low key. I doubt he's going to want to make a big deal of this and try to do a runner. He hardly looks fit enough anyway.'

They left and headed over to where the others had parked. Clem opened the window.

'What's the plan, ma'am?' he said.

'We've spotted him in the café with Whitlock's girlfriend.'

'Two for the price of one,' Billy quipped.

'Yeah, something like that,' she said with a hollow laugh. 'Matt and I will go in there and the rest of you keep the entrances secure to make sure he doesn't try to leave.'

Lauren waited until the others were in place, and then motioned for Matt to follow her into the café. Her heart pounded as they prepared to confront Chief Constable Johnson. She pushed open the door and allowed Matt in first. The café wasn't large and as they approached the table where the chief constable was sitting, he glanced up, alarm written all over his features.

'I'd like you to come with us, please, sir. And you, ma'am,' Lauren said to the woman.

'What for?' Chief Constable Johnson demanded.

'Because we know what's happened.' Lauren kept her voice low and maintained eye contact.

'I don't know what you're talking about,' he protested, his voice rising slightly.

'Let's discuss this back at the station. And don't try to run,' Lauren warned, her gaze flicking to the door to ensure their exit was covered. 'Or you'll both be arrested. Which none of us want. We'd like to keep this as low key as possible.'

'You're not making any sense. Why are you here?' he asked, his confusion seeming genuine.

'Sir, we'll explain everything at the station. Please come with us now.'

'I'm not going with you,' the woman said, a hint of defiance in her voice.

'It's not up for negotiation, Ms Wilde,' Lauren said.

'How do you know my name?' Mandy Wilde said, nervously staring down at her hands. 'There's nothing going on, we're just friends,' she added frantically.

'It didn't look like "just friends" to me,' Matt interjected. 'I believe you were holding hands before we approached.'

Lauren glanced at Matt. Were they? She hadn't noticed – but that put a whole different complexion on things.

'That's got nothing to do with it,' the chief constable said. 'Don't worry, Mandy,' he added softly. 'We can sort all this out. Let's do as the DI asks.'

'Okay,' Mandy said, reluctantly.

'Thank you. Let's walk out together in a friendly manner,' Lauren said, determined to sound in control, despite the whirlwind of thoughts careening around her head regarding how her career was going to be totally wrecked if they'd got this wrong.

'If I'm being interviewed, I want my solicitor,' the chief constable declared in a matter-of-fact tone, as if he was simply ordering a cup of tea.

'That's a very good idea, sir,' Lauren agreed, already several steps ahead, planning their interrogation strategy. 'And the same applies for you,' she said to Mandy, who continued staring at them blankly.

As they escorted the chief constable and Mandy Wilde back to the station, Lauren's thoughts were a whirlwind of what ifs, buts, and maybes. But she was determined to get to the bottom of it.

TWENTY-SIX
THURSDAY, 18 JULY

'Have you decided yet how you want to play this?' Lauren asked DCI Mistry as they headed towards the interview room where the chief constable was waiting for them.

Her steps were measured, trying to match the pace of her boss, who walked much slower than she usually would. Matt walked a couple of paces behind them, intentionally keeping his distance, she suspected. When she'd first informed the DCI that they now had the chief constable in custody, and the circumstances leading to his being brought in, he'd mentioned the possibility of being part of the interviewing team but also said that he needed to think it through before making a final decision. She hadn't realised that he literally meant he wouldn't decide until they were seconds away from the interview.

'It wasn't an easy decision to make but because you know the facts of the case in much greater detailer than me, I'm going to watch you and Sergeant Price from the observation area,' Mistry said without breaking his stride. 'If I'm at all concerned at any point, I'll interrupt. Because of the nature of the case, you're allowed to interview him, despite the differences in rank.'

Lauren tensed, agreeing with his decision although

suspecting that the DCI's absence might make the interview more challenging. 'I think that's the right way to proceed, sir. I'm pleased that you'll be close by should we require your input.'

Upon reaching the interview room, the DCI left them and Lauren took a deep breath, steeling herself for what was to come. The chief constable was seated with his arms folded, exuding an aura of defiance. Next to him sat a highly made-up woman in her early forties, with blonde hair cut in a long bob to her shoulders, who Lauren assumed was his solicitor.

'Good morning,' Lauren said briskly, masking the nerves knotting in the pit of her stomach. 'This interview will be recorded.'

She nodded to Matt, signalling him to start the recording.

'Interview on 18 July,' Matt said, his voice echoing slightly in the sterile room. 'Those present: Detective Inspector Pengelly, Detective Sergeant Price.' He paused, nodding in the direction of the chief constable and his solicitor. 'Please state your names.'

'Rita Holder, solicitor.'

'Warren Norman Johnson,' the chief constable said, avoiding eye contact with Lauren and Matt and staring at a point over their heads.

Lauren wasn't going to be put off by his arrogance. Despite his rank, he was still a suspect in a murder case and that was how she intended to approach the interview.

'Right, sir,' Lauren said, ensuring to use the correct term of address because he was still her superior officer. 'We would like to ask you about the murders of Carmel Driscoll, Jayne Freeman, Craig Garland, and the attempted murder of Nancy Lawson.'

The chief constable finally met Lauren's eyes. 'I know nothing about them,' he replied curtly. His voice betrayed no emotion, but there was a definite stiffening in his posture. A sign of defensiveness?

'We believe that the killing of Ronald Whitlock in a Spanish prison has led to the murder of officers working at Camborne on his case in 1997. You're already aware of this from an earlier interview. We also believe that these murders were orchestrated by Mandy Wilde, who you were seen with at the service station earlier today.'

'That's rubbish. It has nothing to do with her and nothing to do with me.' He banged his fist hard on the table and glared angrily in Lauren's direction.

The solicitor nudged Chief Constable Johnson and he turned to her. She shook her head slightly and he visibly relaxed back into the chair. Had he realised that his behaviour wasn't going to get him anywhere?

'I'm sure you're aware that Wilde was Whitlock's girlfriend and she had a child by him. Whitlock's dead and this child will never get to know his father. Wilde held officers from Cornwall responsible,' Lauren explained, her voice slow and calm, as if talking to a child.

'That's all circumstantial,' the chief constable said defiantly. 'I wasn't responsible for the murder of those officers, and nor was Mandy.' He folded his arms across his chest.

He could deny it all he wanted; Lauren wasn't going to be bamboozled by his behaviour. 'Okay, let's move on,' Lauren said, deciding it was time to shift gears.

'Is it correct that since 1997, if not longer, you've provided vital information to Ronald Whitlock and his gang?'

Panic momentarily shone from Chief Constable Johnson's eyes, but he quickly resumed his previous defiant posture.

Too late, though, because Lauren had witnessed the effect of her words.

'No comment,' he replied tersely.

'And that your contact on the outside is Mandy Wilde,

which is why you were with her today when we arrested you,' Lauren continued, showing no sign of being deterred by his refusal to answer.

'No comment,' he repeated.

Lauren's eyebrows lifted slightly at the response. 'You say that you're innocent, sir, but you're not helping yourself by refusing to answer my questions. You of all people should know that. If you're innocent, as you insist, then I suggest you tell us the truth about why you were with Mandy Wilde today and your involvement with Whitlock over the years.'

'No comment.'

Lauren faked a yawn, as if making out that she found his responses boring.

'Okay, sir. Let's move on to the notes left beside the bodies. Ten green bottles; nine green bottles; eight green bottles... I assume the plan was for them to continue being placed next to future bodies... Although I suspect now there won't be any more. If Wilde is hiring a murderer as revenge for Whitlock's death, then I understand why they were left – except that it was very easy to point the finger once we'd established the link between the deaths and Whitlock's demise. Did Wilde feel so vengeful that being caught didn't matter to her? Why didn't you advise her otherwise?'

'No comment,' the chief constable said, firmly. 'I'm not prepared to answer any more questions. Take me back to the custody suite, if you must, but so far you've provided nothing that amounts to sufficient grounds to charge me with having anything to do with the murders.'

'But we do have grounds. We not only have your involve-ment with Mandy Wilde, the killer has also named you as the person—'

'You can't listen to him. He's saying it out of spite, to push the blame onto anyone other than himself,' the chief constable said, interrupting.

'He? How do you know that the murderer's male?' Lauren asked, arching an eyebrow.

'Um... um... most killers are male. I just assumed...' His sentence hung unfinished in the air.

He was right – and it was not something she could use as evidence against him.

'Well, you assumed right,' Lauren acknowledged. 'But the murderer has nothing to lose by giving us full details of what went down. He was paid to carry out the murders and he's given us names of all those people involved.'

'What do you mean he's got nothing to lose?' the chief constable demanded. 'It's in his interest to implicate others. I suppose the CPS has cut him a deal. Well, I don't care. You can't get me for this because I wasn't involved.'

'I'm sorry, sir, you're already implicated by virtue of the fact that you were with Mandy Wilde when we picked you up. Why were you together?' Lauren asked, leaning forward slightly, and resting her arms on the desk.

The chief constable glanced at his solicitor and then returned his gaze to Lauren. 'No comment.'

He was going to be a hard nut to crack. But she wasn't surprised given the amount he had to lose.

'That's your prerogative, sir. But if you are innocent, then why not tell us what you were doing with Mandy Wilde, and also why you think that the murderer is pointing the finger at you. Is it out of spite?' Lauren suggested, although not really believing it.

'I don't know,' the chief constable said, sounding uncertain. 'It's not clear in my head.'

'Fine. If you're refusing to cooperate then you'll be returned to the custody cells, and we're going to interview Mandy Wilde.'

'She's got nothing to do with it,' he said vehemently.

'Are you saying that because you do?' Lauren retorted, not missing a beat.

'No. I just know, that's all.'

'Well, sir, as I'm sure you'll appreciate, that's not a good enough response. It's our belief that Mandy Wilde and you worked together on this. You provided the names and addresses of the victims, and she arranged to have them murdered. You will wait here until you're escorted back to the custody suite.' Lauren picked up the folder she had in front of her. 'Interview suspended,' she added, as an indication for Matt to stop the recording.

Lauren and Matt left the interview room and encountered DCI Mistry in the corridor.

'You didn't get very far with that,' Mistry observed, with a shake of his head.

'No, sir. We knew he was going to deny it. That's why we need to speak to Mandy Wilde,' Lauren said. 'But first we should search his home and his office, if you can arrange a warrant.'

'I'd rather you leave the office for now and concentrate on his home. At least until we're surer of his involvement.'

'Yes, sir,' Lauren said.

The DCI was probably right, but she'd still have rather have full access to everything.

'Did you notice how protective the chief constable was of Wilde, sir?' Matt asked.

'Yes, I did, and I think that might be his Achilles' heel. You need to exploit it if you're going to get anywhere.'

'The chief constable and Wilde were holding hands under the table until we reached them in the café. They hurriedly released them when they saw us,' Matt said.

'Do you believe that he's in a romantic relationship with her?' Mistry asked, with a frown.

'It's something we need to pursue. Do you wish to observe the interview with Wilde when we get to it?' Lauren asked.

'No, I'll leave that one with you. What are your plans for the chief constable?'

'He can remain in custody. We have at least twenty more hours before we have to charge him or let him go, and that's without requesting an extension. Maybe he'll change his mind by then and assist the inquiry,' Lauren said.

'If only it were that simple,' Mistry mused. 'Remember, Lauren, everything has to be rock solid. Currently all you have is evidence from the murderer. That's not going to hold up in court and I doubt the CPS will be prepared to move forward if that's all we have.'

'Yes, sir.'

'I'll request the search warrant as a matter of urgency. Let me know if you intend to interview the chief constable again, and I'll observe. Also, keep me up to date on Wilde. I have a meeting to attend, but you can fill me in later.'

With that, Mistry walked off and Lauren, together with Matt, continued down the corridor towards the office.

'Thoughts, Matt?' Lauren asked.

'The DCI's right about our evidence not being sufficient to nail the chief constable for his part, even if he does appear to be involved, which I believe he is. But we'll find something. Hopefully there'll be something we can use to link him to the murders when we search his home.'

Lauren let out a long sigh. 'I hope you're right, Matt. I really do. Otherwise he could get away with it.'

TWENTY-SEVEN
THURSDAY, 18 JULY

Driving towards the chief constable's house outside Newton St Cyres, a small village about ten miles from the Devon & Cornwall Police headquarters in Exeter, Matt was struck by the difference in scenery between the two counties. While Cornwall was craggy, Devon was very green. He'd like to explore the area when time allowed.

The chief constable's massive Georgian house was set in some beautiful grounds in the countryside.

'Wow,' Matt muttered. 'He must be earning a packet to be able to afford something like this. It's got to be worth millions. We're never going to be able to search it ourselves.'

'I agree. We'll concentrate on specific areas. His office, for a start,' Lauren said as she brought the car to a halt on the cobbled courtyard beside a large brick triple garage.

On their way to the entrance, Matt double-checked the search warrant in his hand and when they reached the front door, Lauren pulled down on the rope to ring the bell. Moments later, the door was opened by Mrs Johnson.

'Yes?'

'Mrs Johnson, I'm DI Pengelly and this is DS Price. We did actually meet you briefly in your husband's office.'

'Warren isn't at home, if it's him you're after. Actually, I've been phoning him and keep getting his voicemail. I want to check the dinner plans we have for the weekend.'

'May we come in, please. I'm afraid we have something rather delicate to tell you,' Lauren said.

Matt glanced across at the DI. How much was she going to divulge?

She moved to the side and Lauren and Matt stepped into the reception hall, where there was a grand wooden staircase in the middle, and doors leading to different rooms.

'What is it?' Mrs Johnson asked, frowning.

'We have the chief constable in custody at the station for his possible involvement in a serious crime. We have a warrant to search your home,' Lauren said.

Matt held it out for the woman to see.

'W-what's he done?' Fenella asked, faltering.

'I'm sorry I can't divulge that. Is there anywhere you can go while we make our search?'

'Why can't you tell me what he's done? This is ridiculous. He's the *chief constable.*'

Matt exchanged a glance with Lauren. Was the woman going to make it difficult for them?

'It's protocol, I'm afraid, Mrs Johnson.'

'I'll phone Val, his assistant. Will she know?'

'I suspect not,' Lauren stated.

'Okay,' the woman said with a frustrated sigh. 'I'll sit in the garden. Let me know when you've finished.'

'Thank you. Before you go, does the chief constable have an office here?'

'Yes.'

'We'll start our search there, if you could point us in the right direction,' Lauren said.

'I'll take you.' Mrs Johnson led them down a hallway to the rear of the house and stopped outside a door on the left, which she opened. 'I'll leave you to it.'

The office was large, with a bay window providing a panoramic view of the beautifully landscaped rear garden. The antique desk was situated in such a way that he'd be able to observe the vibrant flower beds and stone bird table in the centre of the garden.

'Another grand room,' Matt said. 'I'd spend all my time in here if it was mine. With a bit of luck, we'll find something here and won't have to search any further.'

'Let's take it one step at a time. I'll search the filing cabinet and you can do the desk,' Lauren said.

Matt headed over to the antique desk, which had seven drawers, one in the middle and three either side. He started with the centre drawer, which contained a stapler, paperclips, pencils, and some rollerball pens in black. He then moved to the top drawer on the left and as he rifled through, he came across a stack of printed bank statements. He carefully pulled them out and began scanning the transactions.

'Ma'am, take a look at this,' Matt called out, spreading the statements across the desk. 'These transactions seem odd. Large sums being paid in on a regular basis, but it doesn't say where the money comes from, other than "international transfer".'

Lauren headed over and stared at the statements. 'Interesting. We'll take them with us and ask Ellie to investigate them further. These could be what we need to incriminate him. Good job finding them.'

'He hadn't kept them particularly well hidden. So maybe they're not going to be useful?'

'People tend not to be too careful in their own home and wouldn't even consider that it might be searched. Let's finish up here and have a quick look at the rest of the house.'

Once they'd finished, they headed out to the garden where Fenella Johnson was sitting.

'Did you find what you were looking for?' the woman asked, jumping up when she caught sight of them.

'We've taken some documents with us for further investigation and they'll be returned if we don't need them. Thank you for your cooperation,' Lauren said.

The woman saw them out of the house and waited on the doorstep while Lauren drove down the drive and turned onto the road.

'You know what, I think the bank statements are going to be key,' Matt said. 'Don't ask me how, but I have this feeling.'

'You've changed your tune. But I do hope you're right and it leads to us nailing him,' Lauren said. 'Now let's head back to the station and interview Mandy Wilde.'

* * *

After giving the bank statements to Ellie, Lauren and Matt left to question Mandy Wilde. The woman still hadn't requested a solicitor, despite it being suggested to her.

When they reached the interview room Matt paused, his hand hovering over the handle. He glanced again at Lauren, who nodded for him to open it. He drew in a breath, pushed open the door and they stepped inside the room. He pulled out a chair, which scraped against the floor, and sat next to Lauren, who was opposite Wilde.

'Why am I being held here? Where's Warren?' Wilde asked, staring angrily at Lauren.

Lauren nodded for Matt to start the recording equipment, and he complied. The click of the button seemed loud in the tense atmosphere of the interview room.

'*Warren* – the chief constable – is helping us with our enquiries. You're here because we believe that you were instrumental in the deaths of Carmel Driscoll, Jayne Freeman, and Craig Garland. Also, the—'

'What?' Wilde interrupted Lauren, waving her arm with fierce determination. 'You think I murdered them? That's crazy. I don't even know these people. You can't sit there and accuse me of this.' Her nostrils flared and her dark brown eyes flashed with anger.

She certainly wasn't acting guilty. Instead, her body language indicated frustration at being accused of something for which she was innocent. Then again, if the chief constable had schooled her in how to behave when accused, she could simply be an excellent actor.

Matt was determined to scrutinise every minute expression on her face, to get to the bottom of this.

'If you let me finish,' Lauren said coldly. 'We're not accusing you of actually carrying out the murders, but that you instigated them. You wanted these ex-police officers dead because of Ronald Whitlock being murdered in prison. He's the father of your child and you wanted retribution against those who were responsible for him being extradited to Spain in 1997. The chief constable helped you with this by providing the victims' addresses. You then gave these details to Kevin Dixon and paid him to murder them.' Lauren laid her palms flat on the table and stared directly at Wilde.

'That's ridiculous. I have nothing to do with this. I don't know who this Kevin Dixon is,' Wilde protested, looking first at Lauren and then Matt.

'Yeah right. Dixon's been working with Whitlock's gang for years. A gang that you're a part of, so don't give me that nonsense,' Lauren said with a snort.

Wilde's cheeks flushed a pale pink. She leant forward, placed her elbows on the table and cradled her chin in her palms. 'It's not like that. Yes, Ronnie is the father of my son. But

I've never had anything to do with his gang. You have to believe me. I don't know who this Dixon guy is.'

'No, we don't have to believe you because from where we're sitting it's perfectly clear. You wanted revenge for Ronnie's murder,' Lauren said.

'No, that's not true,' Wilde said, a tremor in her voice.

'Well, tell us what is true then,' Lauren said, sitting back and folding her arms. 'Let's start with why you were in the service station café holding hands with Warren Johnson?'

Wilde glanced down at her lap for a few seconds, her fingers fidgeting nervously. She finally looked back up and sucked in a breath. 'I know this sounds horrible, but when Ronnie died, I was happy because it meant I was free then to be with Warren.'

Matt's eyebrows shot up, and he took a sideways glance at Lauren, who appeared as shocked as he was. He didn't see that one coming.

'So, you and Warren were planning to be together. You do know that he's married, don't you?' Lauren asked, tilting her head to one side, her tone laced with disbelief.

'Yes, of course I do. He's due to retire soon and we'd planned to leave Cornwall and be together.' Wilde sounded calm but her hands were jittery.

'How long have you two been seeing each other?' Matt asked, resting his arms on the table.

'It started with... we've known each other for a long time. He interviewed me when Ronnie was found in Cornwall.' Wilde glanced away from Matt's intense gaze.

Something wasn't right.

'So, you've known him all these years, which means you've also known that he's been providing information to Ronnie and his gang?' Matt pointed out.

'I don't know anything about that.' Wilde clasped her hands together tightly.

'I think you do,' Matt said, staring directly at her trying to pierce through her defence. She was definitely hiding something.

'Look, this has nothing to do with me. All I'm telling you is this: I had nothing to do with the murder of those officers. I wasn't upset when Ronnie died because it meant I now have the freedom to live my own life – with Warren.' Wilde sounded more confident but Matt wasn't buying it.

'That's all very convenient. But then, why would the killer, who we interviewed, incriminate you?' Lauren asked, suspiciously.

'Someone must be setting me up... I'm not speaking any more without a solicitor present.' Wilde's face hardened and she crossed her arms defensively.

Great. Now she decided to clam up. Very convenient.

'That's your choice. You'll remain in custody until such time as we can interview you again with your solicitor,' Lauren said, pushing back her chair and standing.

They remained silent while leaving the interview room and had walked halfway down the corridor.

'Well, ma'am?' Matt asked, his voice echoing slightly in the sparse hallway.

'If what she's saying is true, then what's the motive for killing the officers? Something's missing here that we don't yet know,' Lauren mused. 'Let's get back to the office. Ellie might've come up with something that can help,' she suggested.

'Let's hope so because this interview has left us with more questions than answers,' Matt said, frowning. 'Wilde sounded plausible and her body language did fit with someone telling the truth – like the way her voice cracked slightly when she mentioned her freedom now Whitlock is dead. But... I don't know. It's a very convenient story, isn't it?'

'Yes, it is. But I'm with you. She did appear credible. At least as far as Whitlock and being with the chief constable is concerned...' Lauren paused mid-stride and shook her head grimly before continuing, her hands gesturing emphatically. 'But bloody hell. If that bit's true then the shit will well and truly hit the fan.'

Matt matched her pace, his hands in his pockets. He turned to her. 'Do you think she was telling the truth about not knowing the details of the gang's operations?' he asked, because that certainly didn't ring true for him.

Lauren slowed, her lips pursed in thought. 'It's possible, but unlikely. People in her position often know more than they let on. It's a matter of finding the best way of getting them to talk.'

TWENTY-EIGHT
THURSDAY, 18 JULY

'Matt— I mean, Sarge, quick, over here!' Ellie's voice rang out as he walked back into the office with Lauren.

Matt's heart raced. Could this be the breakthrough they'd been hoping for? He exchanged a quick glance with Lauren before detouring to Ellie's desk. 'What is it?' he asked, unable to hide his excitement.

Ellie leant forwards, her eyes gleaming with the thrill of discovery. 'I've gone through the bank statements you gave me and it led me to some money that the chief constable has in an overseas account,' she explained in a hushed tone.

Matt turned and beckoned for Lauren to come over. 'Ellie's discovered some money belonging to the chief constable,' he said when she reached them. 'Do you want to share this with the team?'

'Yes, they need to know everything,' Lauren said. 'Okay, can I have your attention. We now have something on the chief constable which Ellie will explain. Remember this still stays within the confines of our office.'

Matt and Lauren stepped to the side so that the team could see Ellie.

'Come on, let's nail him,' Billy said, fist pumping the air.

'Enough, Billy,' Lauren warned, giving him a stern look, her lips pressed together in a thin line. 'Remember that Chief Constable Johnson is one of us and we have to tread very carefully.'

'Sorry, ma'am,' Billy conceded quickly, lowering his gaze, and dipping his head in acknowledgement.

Ellie sat upright in her chair and squared her shoulders. A sense of pride swelled within Matt as he reflected on the way she'd gone from being a hesitant newcomer to a self-assured contributor to the team.

'This is what I've found out,' Ellie said, her voice clear. 'The chief constable has had regular payments going into a bank account in the Cayman Islands and he's then transferred some of the money into his personal account in this country at various times.'

The room fell silent, as Ellie's words hung in the air. Everyone exchanged glances, their expressions a mix of shock and disbelief.

'How on earth did you find that out?' Clem said, admiration in his voice.

'It was a case of reverse engineering from the statements Sarge gave me. Although the payments into the account appeared anonymous, I was able to use the numerical codes to find where they originated,' Ellie explained, as if what she'd done was simply routine and not, as Matt very well knew, because of her exceptional talent.

'For how long have payments been going into the overseas account?' Lauren asked, her tone serious.

'Ever since 1997, ma'am,' Ellie replied, her hands clasped in front of her on the desk.

'You mean since Whitlock was imprisoned?' Lauren's lips pursed in thought.

'Yes.' Ellie nodded firmly.

'So, what does that mean?' Lauren said, tapping her fingers on the desk she was standing beside. 'Why pay him from then and not beforehand? What changed in 1997 to trigger those payments? Other than the obvious, that Whitlock was put inside?'

'Maybe Whitlock was keeping him on retainer, to provide whatever information his gang needed,' Matt suggested. 'Perhaps before he went into prison, the chief constable was given cash, but Whitlock didn't want to do that when he was so far away...'

'Yes, that could be it,' Lauren agreed.

'How much money's in there?' Clem asked, leaning forward in his chair.

'Twenty million Cayman Islands dollars,' Ellie revealed, sounding as if she couldn't quite believe the figure herself.

Clem let out a low whistle. 'Blinkin' Nora, that's a lot of money. Almost nineteen million pounds.' He ran a hand through his hair. 'Do you think it's his retirement fund?'

'It certainly could be,' Lauren said, nodding thoughtfully.

'I could retire on a tenth of that,' Billy said, laughing.

'Couldn't we all,' Matt said, with a laugh. 'This is excellent work, Ellie. A fantastic breakthrough.'

'You think?' Billy said in awe, his mouth hanging open slightly with admiration.

'Agreed,' Lauren said, her voice rising above the chatter. 'So that means we can actually link everything back to him, and he hasn't—'

'There's more, ma'am,' Ellie said, interrupting her and holding up a hand.

More? Matt's heart pounded with anticipation. What else could Ellie have found?

'Go on,' Lauren said, holding on to the edge of the desk.

'I tracked the history of the account and found that recently there was a change made. It's no longer in the chief constable's name.' Ellie's voice was matter-of-fact but her eyes betrayed her excitement at the revelation.

'Whose name's on the account now?' Lauren pressed.

'His wife, Fenella, but using her maiden name of Budd,' Ellie revealed.

'Why would he change the name to hers?' Billy asked, his face scrunched up in confusion while he scratched his head.

'I'm guessing that it's so we couldn't trace it back to him. I suspect he was worried that we were getting too close,' Lauren suggested.

'But surely using his wife's name means it wouldn't be that hard to link it back to him,' Jenna added.

'I agree,' Matt said. 'I think there's more to this than simply hiding the money. And another thing. Does his wife know that the money exists and that the name has been changed to hers? Because if she does, then where does it leave Mandy Wilde, who claims to be sailing off into the sunset with the chief constable when he retires?'

'Something's not adding up here. What do we know about the chief constable's wife?' Lauren asked, her brow furrowed in thought.

'During my research into Chief Constable Johnson, I discovered that Fenella Johnson used to be a police officer. That's how they first met. They worked at the same station in Portsmouth. But after they got married and started a family, she gave up work. She hasn't worked since,' Ellie responded, glancing at her screen.

'I see. It's time to re-interview the chief constable, now we have this new information. Hopefully he'll admit to everything. That will make our life a lot easier,' Lauren concluded, a plan clearly forming in her mind. 'Thanks, Ellie.'

'I've never known anyone so good,' Clem said, a grin spreading across his face.

'Me neither,' Billy said, the others nodding in agreement.

The atmosphere in the room was electric with excitement and anticipation.

Ellie blushed and looked down at the desk. 'It's my job,' she said, fidgeting with her hands, clearly uncomfortable with the praise.

'Job be damned,' Clem said, his voice booming with conviction. 'You're an absolute whizz kid. Lenchester's very lucky to have you.' He pointed at Ellie, his expression serious, as if daring anyone to disagree with him. 'Not that Tamsin isn't good, too,' he said, as if feeling guilty.

'Yes, she is. And we'll all be happy when she returns to work because we miss her,' Matt added.

'I don't want you to think I'm trying to take away her job,' Ellie said, looking directly at Billy.

'I might have thought that when you first arrived, but I don't now,' Billy said, giving a hesitant smile, which Ellie returned.

Matt frowned. Was there something going on between the two young officers?

'Jenna, see if you can get hold of the chief constable's solicitor and ask her to come back,' Lauren ordered, cutting across Matt's thoughts. 'We'll still go down to speak to him because he might talk anyway. Clem, contact the custody suite and ask them to take him to the interview room now.'

TWENTY-NINE
THURSDAY, 18 JULY

'Are you okay with all this?' Matt asked Lauren on their way to question the chief constable.

She frowned in his direction. 'What do you mean?'

'This is turning out to be a complex case and although all roads seem to be leading to the chief constable...' He paused, his brow furrowing. 'What if we've got it wrong?' He clenched his jaw, doubt and concern etched across his features.

Lauren stopped in her tracks. 'I've been thinking of nothing else but tried to keep my thoughts to myself in case I worried the team.' She gave a hollow laugh. 'Clearly, I was successful, if you hadn't guessed. We're in too deep to question what we're doing. But if we do have it wrong and our careers go down the pan... we'll leave the force... and become private detectives.'

Matt burst out laughing. 'I can't imagine you wanting to spend your time following cheating spouses...'

'True. So we'd better hope we've got this right,' she said with a determined nod as she resumed walking.

When they entered the interview room, Chief Constable Johnson was seated at the table, his arms folded tightly across his chest and his demeanour intense. He stared directly at them.

'Why am I back here?' the man demanded, his frustration palpable. 'I've already refused to answer further questions.'

'Yes, sir, I do remember you saying that,' Lauren said, ensuring to keep her voice calm and non-emotional. 'But something has come to light and I thought you might like the opportunity of discussing it with us.' She gave a friendly smile, as if she was doing him a favour.

Which of course she wasn't.

Would she ever.

'Well... Okay... but I'm not answering questions without my solicitor.' His resolve appeared to falter for a moment before he masked it with defiance.

'Yes, I did wonder about that, and a member of my team has been instructed to call her. While we're waiting, if you like, you can listen to what we've recently gleaned. This can be off the record until your solicitor arrives. Let's call it a chat,' Lauren offered, hoping that he would take the bait.

'Suit yourself. But don't expect me to comment,' the chief constable said, though his attempt at nonchalance wasn't reflected in his eyes, which betrayed concern.

'Understood. This is about your account in the Cayman Islands,' Lauren began, going straight for the jugular, hoping it might shock him into responding.

She was correct because at the mention of the overseas account, the chief constable paled. 'I don't know what you're talking about,' he said, sounding much less confident than before.

'I think you do, sir. We have a very able researcher on our team, and after being handed the bank statements we recovered from the desk drawer in your home office—'

'What the hell were you doing in my desk. It's private,' he snapped.

'Not when you have a search warrant, *sir*.' She couldn't resist taking a dig.

'Bitch,' he muttered.

'As I was saying,' Lauren said, deliberately ignoring his outburst and keeping her voice light. 'My officer discovered this account, which has twenty million Cayman Islands dollars in it. That's nineteen million pounds, in case you hadn't worked it out. It's a lot of money. More than I'll ever see in my lifetime. What were you planning to do with it? And more to the point, where did it come from?'

'No comment,' Johnson said, clearly struggling to maintain his composure.

Lauren's intuition had been right. The chief constable's reactions, the slight faltering in his voice and the way his eyes shifted... those non-verbal cues spoke volumes. He was hiding something big. And it was up to her to find out what.

She leant forward, staring directly at him until he'd met her gaze. She had his full attention. 'Okay, well, let's put it this way. We know that the account has been in operation since 1997. Very convenient, because that was when Whitlock was sent to prison. Now, it's my assumption – and please correct me if I'm wrong – that you were paid each month for helping Whitlock while he was inside by feeding him and his gang information as and when required. Let's call it a retainer.' She paused, studying his reaction closely.

The chief constable looked away. He was definitely rattled. It was more than a simple denial. There was guilt. Or at least fear.

'Sir, remember, we are off the record,' Matt prompted.

Hopefully that might give the chief constable the push to actually assist them.

'Look, I'm saying nothing. You can't prove the money's mine,' the chief constable finally retorted, his voice tinged with desperation.

'I think the fact that payments were made into your UK account from there and that the account was in your name is proof enough. But what we're also interested in, and maybe you can help: why was the account name recently changed from yours to your wife's?' Lauren stated, calmly.

The chief constable's jaw dropped open, his eyes darkening. 'What the fuck? No way. That can't be,' he spluttered.

Wow... what had they stumbled on? Was the wife doing the dirty on him?

'I'm afraid it is, sir. Recently your name was removed from the account and replaced with your wife's. Didn't you know? That's a lot of money and—'

'You're wrong. No details can be changed without my permission—'

'So you admit it's your account?' Lauren jumped in.

They had him.

The panic had set in. The man's body language screamed disbelief and fear. Lauren was convinced that he had no idea about the name switch. Maybe they could use this to their advantage because from the defeated expression on his face, he looked about ready to divulge what they wanted to know.

All it would take was one small push in the right direction.

'Well, sir, as I've already told you, we have an excellent researcher and she was able to pinpoint the exact date and time the account name was changed to your wife's. I assume this means that you now have no claim on the account,' she concluded, laying out the facts plainly and watching the chief constable's defensiveness shift to outright alarm.

They had him on the back foot. It was time for Lauren to push for the truth.

'I don't believe it. Why would she do that?' the chief constable muttered, staring over their heads, as if his mind was somewhere else.

'You tell us,' Lauren pressed, her voice loud enough for him to start and stare directly at her.

Was he going to admit everything? Something was going

around in his mind. Lauren held her breath whilst waiting for his response.

'Forget it. I'm saying nothing,' the chief constable said, banging the table with his fist.

'Come on, sir. You know what's going to happen if you don't. Do you really want to risk being sent to prison until the case comes to court? Officers don't do well inside. Especially at your rank. Tell us the truth and we'll speak to the CPS about you assisting us.'

Lauren remained silent while he clearly grappled with the situation. Whatever way he looked at it, he was finished. But if he helped them solve the murders, then it could go in his favour.

'Okay, I'll tell you,' he declared, a mix of resignation and defiance in his tone.

Lauren exhaled the breath she'd been holding, absorbing the implication of his sudden willingness to confess.

'Thank you, sir. Are you happy for this to be recorded?' she checked, not wanting to do anything to have him change his mind.

'Do what you want,' he said, waving his arm in a gesture of surrender – or perhaps frustration.

Lauren quickly nodded at Matt to restart the recording. They needed to capture every word while he was still reeling because once calmer, he might not be so cooperative.

'Right, over to you, sir. Please explain what happened. If you could start from the beginning so we can get the timeline right, we would appreciate it,' Lauren said, sounding relaxed and unconfrontational.

The chief constable sighed. 'I was part of the team that caught Whitlock and sent him to prison, as you know. I tried my hardest to sabotage the investigation but couldn't. There was too much evidence against him following the tip-off. But I kept in touch with Whitlock and helped him when I could.'

'How did you become involved with Whitlock in the first

place? When did you start working for him?' Lauren probed, knowing each question led them closer to unravelling the web of corruption.

'I'd known Ronnie for years. When I was working at the Met as a DC, I came across him and we struck up a *relationship*.' He paused. 'I had large gambling debts and couldn't pay them off. Whitlock found out and offered to pay them providing I helped him out every now and again. I had no choice. Me moving to Cornwall was part of the reason why he came down here to hide from the police.'

'Oh...' Lauren said, her mind working ninety miles an hour.

'Unfortunately, it didn't work out and he got sent to Spain.'

'But you continued to be on his payroll while he was in Spain, didn't you?' Lauren asked, ensuring each question was carefully crafted so as to peel away the layers of deceit and to make sure nothing was left out.

'Yes. I fed them what information they needed to continue importing drugs into the country. And there was the human trafficking, too. But those murders... that's something I knew nothing about.'

'The murderer informed us that Mandy was the person who arranged the killings. Did you give her the addresses of the victims?'

'No. I've told you, I knew nothing about the murders.'

'But you could have given the addresses without knowing why they were needed,' Lauren pushed.

'For fuck's sake. Have you got shit for brains, or what? Listen to me, woman. I'm telling you that I knew nothing about the murders and didn't provide any addresses. Women of your rank and above are all the same.'

Wow... What a misogynist... and one with a temper, to boot.

'Seriously, sir. You think talking to me like that is going to help your case?' Lauren said calmly, all the time staring directly at him. 'You might have got away with speaking that way to women in the past, but it's not like that now.'

He stared at her wide-eyed, and she could almost see the cogs going around as he realised what she'd meant.

'I don't know anything about the murders, and I didn't get the victims' addresses. That's the truth,' he said, quietly.

She believed him.

'But what about Mandy? We've been informed that she paid the killer,' Lauren said.

'I don't believe it. She'd never be an accessory to murder, she's too nice a person.'

His voice changed dramatically when discussing the woman. He almost appeared sincere, except Lauren knew what he was really like.

Unless... was he in love with her?

'Despite having a child fathered by a London gangster?' Lauren asked, arching an eyebrow.

'That was an accident and once she became pregnant, she was trapped. But she wasn't involved in any of the gang's activities.'

'That you know of,' Lauren said.

'That, I know. Full stop,' he said adamantly.

'What were you doing together when we picked you up?'

'I wanted to warn Mandy that you were looking into Whitlock's murder and other murders, in case you decided to question her.'

'Mandy told us that she was glad Whitlock was dead because it meant you could be together. Is that correct?' Lauren asked.

The chief constable gave a loud sigh. 'Yes. There's nothing stopping us from being together now. The money you discovered was a retirement fund, for me and Mandy. We planned to live overseas.'

'What about your wife? Did she know that you were on the take?' Matt interjected, leaning forward slightly.

That was a good question. Lauren hadn't even thought to go there.

'Yes, she did,' the chief constable admitted, his gaze dropping momentarily before looking at Matt again.

'What were her thoughts about it?' Matt pressed on.

'Fenella felt the same as me, that there was no way we could get out of the position without risking our family's lives. We decided to make the most of it. She was happy with the lifestyle it gave us.'

'Were you planning to give your wife some money from the Cayman Islands account when you retired?' Matt asked.

The chief constable looked away. 'Ummm...'

That told Lauren everything.

'Did Fenella know about you and Mandy?' she asked.

'I don't think so.'

'If what you're saying is true, that you don't know how come the account details got changed, then is it possible that your wife did it because she found out about you and Mandy?' Lauren suggested.

Her words hung in the air, as the expression on the chief constable's face went from disbelief to shock as he processed Lauren's accusations.

'I suppose she could have done it.' He slumped in his chair. 'But it's not like we have a good marriage. We've led separate lives for years.'

'It certainly didn't seem like that when she popped in during our first interview with you,' Matt said.

'Look, we put on appearances when we have to, but our marriage has been a shell for a long time, so why would she be bothered about me and Mandy?'

'Can your wife access your computer? Does she have all of your passwords?' Matt asked.

'Yes, to both questions.'

Lauren picked up the pen on the desk and twirled it in her fingers while she thought through everything that had been said. It still didn't add up. Were they now dealing with two different issues? First, the murders and second the fact that Fenella Johnson made sure she was able to access the bribes that her husband had been paid over the years by Whitlock's gang. Which put her in the frame.

'So, even if your wife does now have your money, it still doesn't solve the murders,' Lauren said, trying to process it.

'As I've told you ad nauseam, I don't know anything about the murders. Okay, I admit to taking bribes over the years, but not the murders. And I know that Mandy wasn't involved either.'

She wasn't buying it.

'This is what I think happened. You and Mandy Wilde arranged for Whitlock to be murdered and to cover your tracks, you dreamt up this elaborate scheme to murder officers who worked on his extradition to make it look like revenge by the gang he was a part of.'

'Why would I do that?' the chief constable protested. 'Because it would put Mandy in the frame, too.'

'Not if you could provide her with an alibi.'

'You've got it all wrong. Where's your proof?' he demanded, banging his hand on the table.

'We'll find it,' Lauren stated.

'There is none. I've told you everything I know.'

'Who was your contact in the gang while Whitlock was in prison? Who did you give the information to?'

'Joe Budd. He was second in command and stepped up while Whitlock was inside, although he still took orders from him.' The chief constable paused for a moment. 'Maybe all this is down to him because he wanted overall control. He could have employed the man you have in custody to commit the murders and then paid him to incriminate me. You have to check it out. He's my brother-in-law. Fenella's brother, but she doesn't have anything to do with him. They're estranged.'

Fenella *Budd*.

Bloody hell... Could this get any more convoluted?

'We'll look into it,' Lauren said, struggling not to show her surprise at the latest revelation. 'In the meantime, sir, you're going to be charged for working with the gang and taking bribes.'

Even if the chief constable was telling the truth about the murders, it still didn't change the fact that they'd uncovered an officer of the highest rank who had become deeply entangled in a criminal underworld. The press was going to have a field day once that came out. But she couldn't think about that at the moment. For now, they had murders to solve.

'Okay, where are we?' Lauren began, the following morning after she'd returned from a very strained meeting with DCI Mistry regarding the way forward. 'We know from our second interview with the chief constable late yesterday afternoon that he had no idea of the name change on his bank account in the Cayman Islands. In fact, he was stunned and we worked out that it had to be his wife. But we're still no nearer to solving who's behind the murders, if he's to be believed,' she added.

'And do you?' Billy asked.

'The jury's out on that one,' Lauren said with a sigh. 'What's been discovered about Fenella Johnson in my absence?'

'I've been scouring CCTV footage for sightings of her car,' Clem said. 'Last week I tracked her leaving Exeter on the M5 and stopping at a retail park near Taunton. She met a man in the car park and they went inside. We have a photo of him; I'll put it up on the screen.'

'That's Joe Budd, second in charge of the gang, who's actually Fenella Johnson's brother,' Matt said as the image flickered on the screen. 'I checked his record yesterday before leaving.

But the chief constable said they didn't have anything to do with each other.'

'Well, he's clearly wrong about that. How long were they there, Clem?' Lauren asked.

'An hour. After that Fenella Johnson returned to Exeter and Budd headed up north.'

'Excellent work. Is there anything else to report?'

'Yes, ma'am,' Ellie said. 'Payments went from Fenella Johnson's private account into a separate account that I've traced back to Kevin Dixon.'

There was a collective gasp as the realisation of Ellie's discovery hit each one of them.

'Why didn't we find this out sooner?' Lauren snapped.

'Because it wasn't straightforward, ma'am,' Ellie explained, blushing. 'The account was with a different bank and was in Kevin Dixon's daughter's name with him as a signatory. It wasn't until looking into Fenella Johnson's finances that I located the payment to Dixon and made the link. I'm sorry.'

'There's no need to apologise,' Matt said, exchanging a warning glance with Lauren, who needed to remember that Ellie was helping them as a favour and she wasn't a proper member of the team.

'I'm sorry, Ellie. I didn't mean to take it out on you. Matt's right, you've done an amazing job in discovering this. How much was paid into Dixon's account?'

'A hundred and ten thousand pounds. An initial fifty, and then three lots of twenty, one after each of the murders.'

'Surely Dixon must know about the chief constable's wife's involvement because she was the one who paid him,' Billy said, looking puzzled.

'Not necessarily,' Ellie said. 'He might not have recognised the account from where the payments came, if in fact he even checked. He could have assumed he was being paid by Mandy Wilde, or the gang, because he believed the letter that he received came from her. Unless he was told to implicate them.'

'That doesn't make sense because Dixon asked for protection for his wife and child. He wouldn't if it was all a set-up. I'm inclined to believe that he genuinely believed Wilde was paying him,' Matt said.

'I agree, and we need to question him again,' Lauren said. 'But first I want Fenella Johnson brought in. She has everything to gain from this and will currently be thinking that the blame for the murders is falling on her husband and she's in the clear. But being an ex-officer, she'll no doubt be expecting us to interview her. So we won't disappoint. Matt, ask her in for an interview. If she pushes for a reason, tell her it's confidential and we need to speak to her in person. I can't see her refusing because it would seem suspicious.'

'Yes, ma'am.' Matt headed over to his desk, contemplating exactly how they were going to confront Fenella Johnson.

* * *

Matt glanced up as Lauren called him over to her office. 'Yes, ma'am?' he said.

'Fenella Johnson's here. Let's go. Follow my lead; I want to keep it low key and then make our move when she least expects it.'

'Okay, ma'am,' he said.

They headed down to the interview room, where Fenella Johnson was already waiting. The room was simply furnished, with a single table and three chairs, one of which was occupied by their suspect. A dim light flickered above, casting long shadows that seemed to stretch across the cold, grey walls.

'Good morning, Mrs Johnson,' Lauren said cheerfully, clearly attempting to put the woman at her ease.

'Hello, Detective Inspector. I was surprised you wanted me

in and didn't come to the house to interview me. But please call me Fenella.'

'Thanks, Fenella. We've asked you in so that we can record the interview. It needs to be more official. I'm sure you understand,' Lauren said, playing it down.

Matt leant across the table and started the recording equipment.

'Of course,' Fenella said. 'Ask me whatever you want. I assume this is about Warren. He didn't come home last night, so I'm guessing he's still in custody.'

'Yes, he is. The crime he's being charged with goes back over thirty years. He was being bribed by a London gang. But you already know this, don't you?' Lauren said, her words sounding more like a statement than a question.

Fenella lowered her head, as if ashamed. 'Yes. I did know. After we were married, I overheard him on the phone to someone and confronted him. He told me all about it. By that time, he was in too deep to stop because we'd be in danger. But that's as far as my knowledge went. I kept well out of it after that.'

'Didn't you think he should stop?' Matt asked.

'It didn't matter what I thought. In the end I put it to the back of my mind,' she responded, her hands clasped together in her lap.

She was certainly putting on a good act.

'And, of course, there's the account in the Cayman Islands,' Lauren said.

Fenella gasped audibly, her face turning ashen. 'What account?' she said, clearly feigning ignorance.

'Let's not play games, Fenella. You do know about this account because recently the name on the account was changed from your husband's to yours, and it was you who did it,' Lauren said.

'That's not true. I don't even know about this account. I've got nothing to do with this. I came here to help you and now you're accusing me. I'm not answering any more questions.'

Her words sounded genuine but there had been a subtle change in the woman's demeanour. Her eyes had hardened and her tone had become more defensive. But whether she'd crack and admit everything remained to be seen.

'Fine. You sit there and I'll talk,' Lauren said, glancing at Matt and arching an eyebrow.

Fenella Johnson was refusing to answer questions but she hadn't asked for a solicitor, which meant they could carry on.

'Do what you want,' Fenella said, her voice cold.

'We believe you found out about your husband's affair with Mandy Wilde, and that he was planning to leave you and go overseas using the money from the account in the Cayman Islands. That would have left you on your own, with no financial support. And that is why *you* were the one to change the name on the account. It was nothing to do with him. How am I doing so far?' Lauren asked, her focus never leaving the woman.

'No comment,' Fenella said, flatly.

'But that wasn't enough for you. You wanted revenge, so you contacted your brother Joe Budd and decided between you to get rid of Whitlock in prison, leaving Budd in control of the gang, and kill the officers involved in his extradition and set up your husband and Mandy Wilde. You employed Kevin Dixon to carry out the murders, letting him believe that his orders came from Wilde.'

'That's ridiculous,' Fenella said, looking away. 'I don't know who this Dixon is.'

'Really?' Lauren said, a deadpan expression on her face. 'Then please explain why you paid him one hundred and ten thousand pounds from one of your bank accounts. We know of your involvement, so there's no point in denying it. Your husband's going to be prosecuted for taking bribes. Kevin Dixon won't get to court because he's got cancer, but we have everything we need to charge you now. What we're suggesting is you give us a statement, plead guilty, and at least then the CPS might look more favourably on you.'

Fenella Johnson's body tensed and her hands gripped the edges of the table. 'I've spent over thirty years with Warren, putting up with him and his affairs. And believe me, this wasn't the first. I stayed because I knew that when he retired, we'd have a decent life. And then I discovered what he was planning. I wouldn't mind, but it's thanks to me that we have this money and—' She stopped mid-sentence.

Now it was all coming out.

'Explain?' Lauren asked. 'Your husband informed us that it was because Whitlock paid off some debts and that's how he got involved with him.'

'After *I* told Joe the trouble Warren had got himself in, and Joe then told Ronnie,' she spat.

'You mean the gambling debts?' Matt asked, still not grasping the situation entirely.

'Yes. Because Warren's such an idiot.'

'So when you told us that you only discovered the bribery because you overheard your husband on the phone, it was a lie?' Lauren asked.

'Yeah. So what.'

'How did you find out your husband was intending to take off with Mandy Wilde?' Matt asked, focusing directly on her, the faint hum of the interview room's fluorescent light filling the brief silence.

'I saw some texts on his phone between the two of them. His phone was on the side when he was in the shower, and I decided to look through it. That was when I made up my mind what to do. I got in touch with Joe and we came up with the plan.' She shrugged nonchalantly.

'You're admitting to instigating the murders of three innocent ex-police officers simply because you didn't want to be poor in your retirement,' Matt growled.

'Collateral damage. It happens,' the woman said coldly.

Matt exchanged a look with Lauren. The woman was beyond belief. She was showing no remorse about the deaths at all.

'What about the emails and the notes left beside the bodies? Was that all down to you?'

'Well, Joe doesn't know one end of a computer to another.'

'What was the point?'

'To lead you to Warren and that woman.' A callous sneer crossed the woman's lips. 'Ingenious, if I say so myself.'

'Does that mean you know all about these Tor networks?' Matt asked.

'It's not hard.'

'And Whitlock's murder?'

'Part of the plan.'

'Fenella Johnson, I'm arresting you on suspicion of being an accessory to the murders of Carmel Driscoll, Jayne Freeman, Craig Garland, and the attempted murder of Nancy Lawson. You do not have to say anything, but it may harm your defence if you do not mention when questioned something which you later rely on in court. Anything you do say may be given in evidence,' Lauren said, reciting the woman's rights with ease. 'I'll fetch someone to take you into custody,' she concluded and left the room.

'You think I'm mad, don't you?' Fenella said to Matt as they sat in silence waiting for Lauren to return.

'It doesn't matter what I think,' Matt replied, his voice low. 'You're going down for a long time.'

The door opened, and Lauren appeared again with an officer. 'Please take Mrs Johnson to the custody suite and charge her,' she instructed.

'What about Joe Budd?' Matt asked, when they were alone.

'I've instructed uniform to bring him in. Who'd have thought that at the start of the day we'd have had this case all wrapped up? Not me, for sure,' Lauren said, beaming widely.

'Me neither,' Matt agreed. 'But what a waste of life just because of one woman being intent on revenge against her cheating husband.'

'It was more than that, Matt. But I agree. It's crazy the depths to which desperation and revenge can drive a person.'

After going out for a walk to clear his head, Matt noticed an unusual congregation around Ellie's desk. His gaze sharpened, and he spotted Tamsin there, sitting on a chair with her leg outstretched. A mix of concern and curiosity bubbled up inside him as he made his way over.

'Hey, Tamsin. How're you doing?'

'Well, as you can see, not so well,' Tamsin replied, her voice carrying a hint of resignation. 'I'm going to be off work for at least another six weeks, if not longer. I have to rest my leg and, once it's a bit stronger, have physio.'

'How did you get here?' Matt asked, his eyebrows knitting in concern.

'I asked my dad to bring me in. I wanted to catch up with everyone to see how it's all going. I'm so bored at home. There's only so much daytime telly a person can watch without succumbing to brain rot. And all my gaming partners are working.'

'I don't know, a few days watching nothing but TV would be a welcome change, I reckon,' Billy said, with a grin.

'Try it and then comment,' Tamsin said, scrunching up her

face. 'Anyway, Sarge, I hear that congratulations are in order. You solved *another* murder case.'

'Yeah, that's right,' Matt acknowledged.

'I can't believe I missed all the excitement. Will you be celebrating? Because I'm sure you can convince me to have a drink, even if it is only a soft one.' Tamsin chuckled.

'I'm sure we will be later,' Matt said.

'We've missed having you around, Tamsin, but Ellie here's done a grand job in your absence,' Clem said.

'Yes, so I hear,' Tamsin said, turning to look at Ellie, who appeared to be trying to blend into the background.

'It's nothing,' Ellie said, her voice barely above a whisper, clearly downplaying her achievements.

'Honestly, no offence to you, Tamsin, but Ellie's work has to be seen to be believed. I don't think she's human,' Billy joked, breaking the tension.

He turned and winked in Ellie's direction and she blushed.

'Don't be silly,' Ellie protested, but her words were lost in the laughter that had erupted.

'You'll get used to Billy in time – I did,' Tamsin said good-naturedly.

'I think she already has,' Jenna added, with a smirk. 'He's taking her sightseeing tomorrow morning.'

Had Billy and Ellie struck up a friendship already?

Or even more?

'I'm glad you were here to help solve the case, Ellie. I felt so guilty for being off work.'

'Well, who told you to go out skateboarding when you were drunk?' Clem teased, sparking another round of laughter.

'Look, I'll be as old as you one day but for now I want to enjoy myself. I was out having fun, that's all. I didn't know it would turn out quite like this,' Tamsin retorted. 'And I'm sure it's much worse for me than it is for you, being stuck at home all day with nothing to do. So, you should be feeling sorry for me,' she added, a playful glint in her eye.

'We definitely feel sorry for you,' Matt said, his voice warm with genuine concern and affection. 'Anyway, it's a bit early to go out for an after-work drink, but we'll certainly have something to celebrate later.'

As the laughter died down, Matt scanned the room, staring at his colleagues one by one, a sense of camaraderie and gratitude washing over him. Despite the setbacks and challenges, they were a team, and that's what mattered most.

'You know what, Sarge? If I'm away from the office for some time, why don't you see if Ellie can stay here with us?' Tamsin suggested, a hopeful note in her voice.

'Would you like that, Ellie?' Jenna asked.

'I mean, you seem to have enjoyed yourself here, and it's certainly a change from being stuck in Lenchester,' Tamsin said.

'You're right, I have enjoyed myself working here,' Ellie admitted, tossing a hurried glance in Billy's direction.

Was she serious? Did she really want to stay here for a while? Though quite how Whitney would react to the request remained to be seen.

'Is it possible, Sarge? Can Ellie be seconded here until Tamsin comes back to work?' Billy asked.

'It won't be that easy,' Ellie interjected. 'I'm needed back at Lenchester.'

'But surely you can ask your boss if they can spare you. It's a big force. There must be loads of people to take your place. It's not like here when if we're one down, it's really noticeable,' Tamsin pressed.

'I would like to,' Ellie said, her gaze meeting Matt's for a moment. 'Except...'

'What?' Tamsin asked.

'Where would I stay? I can't afford to live in a bed and breakfast.'

'That's not a problem. You can stay with me. My flatmate has been sent overseas with work for six months. Her room's available and it won't cost you a thing,' Tamsin said.

'Are you sure?' Ellie asked, her face lit up with excitement.

'Yes. Of course,' Tamsin said, enthusiastically. 'All you'll have to do is contribute towards the bills and—'

'Hang on a minute,' Matt interrupted. 'Before you go any further with the plans, I'll ask the DI if it's possible. Obviously, we'll also need to speak to DCI Walker as well. But, if you want to do this, Ellie, and it can be arranged, we'd love to have you here. You've settled in very well.'

'Thanks, Sarge,' Ellie responded, a hesitant smile playing at the corner of her lips.

Matt left the team and made his way to Lauren's office. He knocked on the door, his heart pounding slightly with anticipation.

'Come in,' she called.

'Got a minute, ma'am?' Matt asked as he entered, closing the door behind him.

'Yes. I'm finishing the admin on the case,' Lauren answered, her attention momentarily shifting from her paperwork to Matt.

'Have you seen that Tamsin's here?'

'I did catch sight of her and was going to say hello once I'd finished this. How is she?'

'She's fine but going to be off for the next six weeks. The team has come up with a suggestion which Ellie agreed to and I said I'd run past you. They thought that maybe Ellie could get a secondment down here for a couple of months while Tamsin's recovering,' Matt said, trying to gauge Lauren's reaction as he relayed the proposal.

'It's a great idea, Matt. Providing Tamsin's okay with it, of course. I don't want her upset by it.'

'She's fine. It was mainly her idea.' Matt added, hoping to underscore the mutual agreement among the team.

'They've really taken to Ellie,' Lauren mused, a hint of approval in her tone.

'Especially Billy by the looks of things. Which considering how he was at first is a surprise. I wouldn't be surprised if they become more than colleagues.'

Lauren frowned. 'I'm not sure about that. Relationships in the workplace can be problematic.'

'Look, this is only my view from observing their friendship forming. Anyway, she's only going to be here for a couple of months, so nothing for us to worry about.'

'What do you think DCI Walker will say about the suggestion?' Lauren asked.

'She knows Ellie's been having a tough time recently, so she may agree. Would you like me to ask her?'

'No, it should come from me,' Lauren said.

'I'll forward you her number,' Matt said, taking out his phone.

'Well, no time like the present. I'll put her on speaker, then you can speak, too,' Lauren suggested, as she pressed the number which was answered almost immediately.

'DCI Walker.'

'Hello, it's DI Lauren Pengelly from Penzance, and I've got Sergeant Matthew Price with me. You're on speaker.'

'Hi, Matt, how are you?' Whitney said, warmly.

'I'm great, thanks. How about you?' Matt responded, smiling.

'Non-stop, as usual. Are you phoning about Ellie? Is everything okay?' Whitney asked, sounding concerned.

'Yes, it's fine,' Matt said. 'She's been helping us with a case because our usual researcher had a skateboarding accident and is off sick for the next six weeks.'

'Oh my goodness. I'm assuming Ellie's done okay. I mean, she is incredible.'

'Yes, we've discovered that for ourselves,' Lauren said.

'That's why I'm phoning. We wondered if you would consider us having DC Naylor on secondment for a couple of months until Tamsin, my DC, is back at work.'

'I see,' Whitney said, her voice non-committal. 'Is this what Ellie wants, Matt?'

'Yes, she's really keen. It might be good for her after the split with Dean and her granddad's passing. She's already more relaxed than when she arrived. Is it going to be a problem?'

'I suppose we can make it work, if that's what she wants. But we'll miss her, for sure. We'll need to go through the proper channels, which is bound to be an HR headache.' Whitney gave a hollow laugh. 'Leave that with me. But it doesn't mean I don't want her back when Tamsin returns.'

'I will have to get permission from my DCI, but I don't envisage any issue. Thank you, DCI Walker,' Lauren said.

'Please, call me Whitney.'

'You're my superior officer,' Lauren said with a frown.

'Well, that's as may be, but call me Whitney. And I hope you enjoy working with Ellie. You've got Matt already, so please don't go after any more of my guys.' Whitney laughed.

'Understood,' Lauren said.

'Matt, it's been ages since I've seen you. Are you planning on coming up for a visit?' Whitney asked.

'I'm not sure. Maybe you should come down here for a holiday. Bring Tiffany and Ava,' Matt suggested.

'I'll think about it. I could certainly do with a break. It's been lovely speaking with you both, but I do have a meeting to attend with Dic—' She cleared her throat. 'I mean Superintendent Douglas.'

Matt laughed. 'Some things don't change.'

They ended the call, and Lauren turned to Matt, who was still smiling to himself at Whitney's comment. 'An *in joke*?'

'Between the two of us, Superintendent Douglas's nickname is *Dickhead Douglas*. Whitney and he both go back a couple of decades. It's a long story.'

'Which I don't need to know. But that aside Whitney seems okay.'

'I've always said she was. You both operate in very different ways. But ultimately want the same thing. To get the job done at all costs. That's why I enjoy working with you so much. And want to stay here for the foreseeable future. I'm going back to the office to let Ellie know the outcome. Are you going to join us for a celebratory drink later?'

'Definitely. We also need to fix up a time for Dani to see the dogs. Are you around tomorrow morning – we could go to the park?'

'Yes, I was going to mention that. Tomorrow would be great. Ellie's out with Billy, so she won't need entertaining. We'll meet you at ten at our usual spot.'

'Look, there's Lauren,' Dani said, jumping up from the bench she was sitting on with Matt.

He glanced in the direction his daughter was staring and saw Lauren with the two dogs by her side. Dani ran towards them and Matt hurried behind, trying to keep up.

'I'm so sorry to be late,' Lauren said, when they reached her. 'It was all go this morning. I popped into work early to do a couple of bits before meeting you and my phone was going non-stop.' She seemed frazzled, and stressed. 'Hello, Dani. How are you now?'

'Very well thank you,' Dani recited, as Matt's mum had taught her.

'Okay, you two. Sit,' Lauren said to the dogs, who immediately obeyed the command. 'Dani, if I let the dogs off the lead, are you going to play with them carefully?' Lauren's tone was both caring and cautious.

'Yes.' Dani beamed, looking at the dogs with excitement.

'Make sure to stay close to us and don't go running off, even if Ben and Tia do,' Matt added firmly.

'I won't, Daddy.'

'I have two balls,' Lauren said, handing them to Dani. 'Throw them for the dogs and they'll bring them back to you.'

Dani threw the balls one at a time as hard as she could, which was only a couple of metres. The dogs joyfully bounded after them, running back to Dani, and dropping them at her feet and making her giggle.

Matt's heart felt fit to burst. Dani's happiness was everything to him.

'They're very well-trained,' Matt remarked.

'They are good. Especially when they're with Dani. You know how much they love her,' Lauren said, smiling warmly. The affection she had for his daughter was clearly genuine. 'Shall we sit down,' she said, gesturing to a bench close by.

'So, what's been going on at work?' Matt asked, once they were seated.

'I had a phone call from the prison where Kevin Dixon's being held. He's taken a turn for the worse and is going into a hospice over the weekend. They think he's only got a matter of weeks left.'

'Oh dear, that's a shame. What about his wife and daughter?' The man was a murderer but that didn't mean his family should suffer.

'Social services have been informed, and they'll make sure the family is looked after. Obviously, he wasn't able to keep the money that he was paid, but they should be fine,' Lauren explained.

'It's going to be hard for them,' Matt said, a pang of empathy hitting him. He knew all too well how hard losing a partner could be, even more so, he imagined, because of the daughter's disability. He glanced at Dani, who was now playing happily with the dogs, feeling grateful for their stability.

'Very,' Lauren agreed.

'What else happened?' Matt prompted.

'I had a chat with the DCI regarding the chief constable.

Obviously, the higher-ups are all in total shock that he could have done what he did for so many years. There's going to be a public inquiry. Top brass is also planning to hold a press conference to give the official line, because once the media gets hold of this story, it could run and run.'

'Yeah, you're not wrong about that. What about his past history and the harassment charges? Do you think the cases should be reopened, especially as Nancy Lawson could speak out about his behaviour?'

'It would be very difficult because two of his accusers are now dead and she left before the investigation. We have to be thankful that he's going to end up in prison for the bribery.' Lauren shook her head slightly. 'But... details of his past might slip out in a media briefing.'

'Good,' Matt said adamantly. 'He deserves his comeuppance for what he did.'

'Absolutely,' Lauren agreed, her expression hardening.

'One thing I was thinking,' Matt said. 'With Fenella Johnson, Joe Budd and Whitlock out of the picture, where does that leave the gang?'

'I've no idea. But I suspect losing their number one, number two, and their police informant, they'll be lying low for a while. No doubt they'll—'

'Daddy, Daddy!' Dani's excited voice as she ran over to them interrupted their conversation.

'What, sweetheart?' Matt asked.

'I taught Tia to high-five!' Dani exclaimed, her face beaming with pride.

'Really? How did you manage to do that?' Matt asked, genuinely impressed.

'I don't know, I said "high-five" and she did it,' Dani explained, excitedly.

'Well done,' Lauren said. 'Now, do you think you can teach them to wipe their feet before they come in from outside? It would make the house so much cleaner. Or maybe to ring a bell when they want to go out. It would save me having to leave the back door open when it's cold.'

'I don't know, but I can try,' Dani said earnestly.

'Excellent. Right, why don't we get an ice cream from the van over there,' Lauren proposed, pointing towards the road.

'Good idea. I'll have a 99,' Matt responded.

'Can I have one, too, Daddy, please?' Dani asked, hopping from foot to foot.

'If they do a small one, of course,' he said.

Watching Dani's joy and Lauren's caring nature, which so often she kept hidden, a wave of contentment washed over him. As they headed towards the ice cream van, he was grateful for these odd moments of normality amidst the chaos that was so much a part of his life.

A LETTER FROM THE AUTHOR

Dear reader,

Huge thanks for reading *The Camborne Killings*. I hope you enjoyed returning to Lauren and Matt's world once again for this new case. If you want to join other readers in hearing all about my new books, you can sign up here:

www.stormpublishing.co/sally-rigby

If you enjoyed the book and could spare a few moments to leave a review that would be hugely appreciated. Even a short review can make all the difference in encouraging a reader to discover my books for the first time. Thank you so much!

I had an absolute ball writing this book, delving into the murky depths of police corruption, treachery, and the sort of retribution that creeps up on you when you're least expecting it. Keeping readers on the edge of their seats wondering who was guilty or innocent was such fun. And the twist at the end? That was like the proverbial icing on the cake.

Thanks again for being part of this amazing journey with me and I hope you'll stay in touch – I have so many more stories and ideas to entertain you with!

Sally Rigby

KEEP IN TOUCH WITH THE AUTHOR

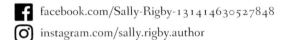

facebook.com/Sally-Rigby-131414630527848

instagram.com/sally.rigby.author

ACKNOWLEDGEMENTS

First and foremost, I want to express gratitude to my amazing editor, Kathryn Taussig, for her invaluable insights, meticulous attention to detail, and unwavering support throughout the entire process. Her guidance and expertise have been instrumental in shaping this novel into its final form. I also extend my thanks to the talented editing, cover design, marketing, and production staff for their hard work and dedication in bringing this book to life. Thanks also to Oliver Rhodes, without whom Storm wouldn't exist, and by default, nor would this book.

I am grateful to my incredible advanced reader team for generously giving their time to read early drafts of this novel. Your feedback, encouragement, and enthusiasm have been truly inspiring and have helped me refine the story in countless ways.

Thanks, also, to my family for your continued support.

Printed in Great Britain
by Amazon